v

The Vengeance Man

The Vengeance Man

John Dean

ROBERT HALE · LONDON

ISBN-10: 0-7090-7994-X
ISBN-13: 978-0-7090-7994-1

Robert Hale Limited
Clerkenwell House
Clerkenwell Green
London EC1R 0HT

2 4 6 8 10 9 7 5 3 1

Typeset in 11/13½pt Palatino
Printed in Great Britain by St Edmundsbury Press
Bury St Edmunds, Suffolk.
Bound by Woolnough Bookbinding Ltd

CHAPTER **ONE**

'In my experience,' said John Blizzard, reaching for his mug of tea without looking up from the report he was reading, 'arresting the undead can be a tricky business. Even when you get them in a cell, they walk right through the wall. Drives the custody sergeant spare.'

Detective Sergeant David Colley, sitting on the other side of the desk, grinned broadly, enjoying the detective chief inspector's joke. Not so the butt of their humour. Detective Inspector Chris Ramsey sat next to the sergeant, glumly wishing he were somewhere else than Blizzard's office at Abbey Road Police Station. Unlike the chief inspector, Ramsey had worked the weekend and was already weary and in no mood for Blizzard's humour as they held their Monday morning briefing.

'And what would you charge him with?' asked Blizzard, warming to his theme. 'Going against the spirit of the law, I imagine.'

Ramsey did not smile. A conscientious, thorough and precise – some would say over-precise – man, he was not noted among his colleagues for his levity. His silence caused Blizzard to look up and survey him for a moment. And despair. Aged in his early thirties, Ramsey was slim and tall with short-cropped brown hair, an angular face, a prominent nose and a thin mouth not particularly given to laughing. A dour man, that morning he was dressed as immaculately as ever, in a grey suit with a perfectly matching powder-blue tie, and black shoes. Whatever you said about Chris Ramsey, reflected Blizzard, who was not noted for his sartorial elegance, he was always well turned out.

The DI returned the chief inspector's gaze without much warmth. It had been like this ever since, three weeks ago, he had mentioned the strange goings-on in Heston, once a small fishing village but now a rapidly-expanding and well-heeled suburb on the western tip of the sprawling Hafton conurbation. The jokes had come thick and fast once it emerged that the DI was investigating a phantom. Particularly irritating to the DI, who had never been one for banter, was the young uniformed constables who kept making 'whooing' noises whenever he walked past them in the corridor. That was irritating enough but what irked Ramsey most was the refusal of Blizzard to take the matter seriously. As a senior detective, Ramsey felt he deserved better from his boss.

'Sorry, Chris,' said Blizzard, dismally failing to keep a straight face as the DI glowered at him, 'but I don't reckon you have a ghost of a chance with this one.'

'Oh, for God's sake, sir!' exclaimed Ramsey in exasperation.

'Keep your hair on, Chris.' said the chief inspector quickly, realizing that he had gone too far with his banter. 'It's only a joke.'

For all his approach to the inquiry, Blizzard had actually quite welcomed it. Chris Ramsey's investigation had provided light relief amid the usual doom and gloom of life in Hafton's Western Division. It had all started when a shaken young man arrived at the little police office in Heston market place in the early hours of the morning and, having banged frantically on the front office reception window for some minutes, announced to the startled desk sergeant that he had seen a ghost. The sergeant, recognizing him as a local drug user, had tried to send him on his way with a dismissive flap of the hand but the young man was adamant and refused to leave so a report was duly filed. Once dispatched to divisional headquarters at Abbey Road, it ended up on an intrigued Chris Ramsey's desk.

And strange reading it made, too. According to the young man, he had been taking drugs in the graveyard in Heston. The drug users liked the graveyard behind the thirteenth-century parish church because it was rarely used for burials and few people visited, the space for new plots having long since run out. Indeed, the last person to be buried there was interred in the 1950s. The graveyard's secluded position, away from the market place and the surrounding terraced streets, had made it a popular meeting place for local drug takers but now, if the junkie was to be believed, and Ramsey and his colleagues usually tended not to believe them, someone, something, wanted them out.

According to the teenager, he was alone, spaced out and having a lie-down on one of the overturned gravestones at about midnight when, silently from out of the shadows, there emerged a tall figure. Although it was very dark, the druggie could nevertheless see, faintly illuminated by the nearby street lights, that the man wore a long dark coat and boots. The addict could not see his face beneath the wide brim of his hat, something that added to his terror and that he repeated several times in his statement. But for all that, what he remembered most was the voice. Rasping, the boy's statement said. Menacing. Scary. Reading the report, Chris Ramsey could almost sense the young man's fear.

As the teenager sprawled in horror, the stranger had walked towards him, jabbed a threatening finger in his direction and warned him that he should stop taking drugs in the graveyard. Then, without any further sound, the stranger had disappeared back into the shadows, leaving the teenager cowering on the gravestone. Once he had gathered what little of his drug-addled senses remained, the boy had run for his life, badly gashing his leg as he scrambled over the graveyard railings and narrowly avoiding a speeding taxi as he tumbled into the street. The driver had been traced and confirmed that he had to swerve to avoid the teenager, who had fled the other way down the street in fear of his life. A medical examination confirmed the presence of a gash on the boy's leg.

It was a bizarre incident and one that left Chris Ramsey bemused. Normally, he would have been tempted to consign it to the 'strange-but-true' file were it not for the fact that it was repeated a couple of weeks later when another glassy-eyed drug user, staggering out of the churchyard at half past midnight, heard a noise and peered back into the darkness. The figure once more emerged from the shadows. He wore the same long coat, boots and hat and again the boy could not see the face. It was a fact that had made a big impression on both witnesses. As had the voice, the stranger warning the teenager to stop taking drugs in his graveyard before melting once more into the shadows.

Shocked and frightened, the teenager had scuttled from the graveyard, colliding with gravestones and slipping on the wet grass more than once. Despite himself, he had glanced back when he reached the wrought iron gate to see, to his horror, that the figure was pursuing him, appearing to tower above the railings and eerily illuminated in the orange glow of the street lights as he pointed an accusing finger. The teenager had not looked back again and had headed to the police station where the same desk sergeant dutifully filled out a report, convinced that the boy had suffered some kind of drug-induced hallucination.

Again, the report wound its way on to Ramsey's desk and by this time the DI was feeling thoroughly uneasy about the whole affair, unwilling to regard it as a simple prank despite the comments of fellow officers. Blizzard, for his part, continued to ignore his colleague's protestations and dismissed it as the actions of a crank, placing it low down on the priority list for Western Division. Ordinarily, Ramsey would have been tempted to agree; he had, after all, met Jesus Christ (nice bloke if somewhat scruffy and with a somewhat un-Christian penchant for Carlsberg lager) and Napoleon (an unpleasant character who seemed unwilling to wash) during his time as a police officer. But, unimaginative as some would say Chris Ramsey was, there was something about the addicts' stories that sent shivers down his spine.

Sure, he told himself, both witnesses were drug-takers, and probably perfectly capable of hallucination and fabrication, but there was something very real about their testimonies. And why come voluntarily to the police and admit to having taken drugs, risking arrest and prosecution, when they could have kept silent? No, something had driven them to seek out police help and that made a great impression on a DI more used to evasive addicts who would run a mile rather than co-operate with a police officer.

Although Ramsey had been extremely busy overseeing Western CID's huge routinely heavy workload – mainly burglaries, robberies, assaults and auto-crime – as well as battling the mountain of paperwork that accompanied them, the detective inspector had nevertheless found time to visit both drug users at their homes and found them extremely convincing when they told their stories. Blizzard, however, had remained less convinced, his attention focused on more earthly considerations, which is why he had not been particularly encouraging when Ramsey raised the matter again at their daily morning meeting.

'I'm sorry, Chris,' the chief inspector said, laughter banished as he noticed his DI's growing irritation, 'but I can't really take this seriously and, frankly, you've got too much else to do without chasing ghosts.'

'Yes, I know b....'

'What about those shop robberies, for a start? There was another one over the weekend and this time they coshed the shopkeeper.'

'I know, I was out t....'

'They're becoming more violent and the super is

demanding some answers,' and Blizzard looked hard at the DI. 'As, frankly, am I.'

'I know, I know,' nodded Ramsey, holding up a file, 'but this graveyard thing isn't going away, sir. We had another report in Heston last night.'

'Another drug taker?'

'Yeah. He was shooting-up in the cemetery when this "thing" appeared and threatened him.'

'Threatened?'

'Said vengeance would be his. I just think we should be doing a bit more to find this guy, sir. What if he's dangerous?'

'Oh, come on, Chris!' exclaimed Blizzard. 'He's obviously a nutter and, to be honest, if he's putting the wind up some of the local junkies who am I to complain? Besides, thanks to this stomach bug going round we're short-staffed this week. You know that.'

'I know,' nodded Ramsey, who had been forced to cancel his days off because of the crisis, disappointing his five-year-old daughter to whom he had promised a visit to the park. 'It's just I've got a bad feeling about this one.'

'And I've got a bad feeling about the super asking me what we are doing about the robberies – and he's got a bad feeling about the chief constable taking a keen interest in them, so I don't want you wasting any more time on it.'

'There's another thing....' said Ramsey tentatively.

'Don't tell me,' said Blizzard acerbically, winking at David Colley, 'the Loch Ness Monster has started eating Jack Russells on the riverbank.'

The sergeant, who had been leaning back in his chair, silently enjoying the exchange, allowed himself a smile but quickly wiped it from his face when Ramsey glared at him.

'No, sir,' said the DI, 'The local newspaper stringer in Heston has got hold of the story. He rang me first thing, the paper is going big on it tonight apparently.'

'Just what we don't need,' sighed Blizzard, whose

dislike of reporters was legendary. 'It'll be a bloody media circus now.'

His phone rang and he listened grim-faced for a moment or two, glanced at Ramsey, then grunted, 'Tell them we're investigating.'

He put the phone down.

'Bring on the clowns' he sighed. 'That was the press office about your flipping ghost. You were right, the local rag has asked for a comment.'

'Do I assume from what you told them that I can investigate then?' asked Ramsey hopefully.

'Yes,' replied the chief inspector without much enthusiasm. 'But I don't want you wasting too much time on it. This isn't sodding Scooby Doo.'

Colley chuckled but was silenced by another glare from Ramsey.

'And I'm only letting you do it to keep the press office happy,' warned Blizzard. 'I don't want it getting in the way of your inquiries into these robbers. They're a nasty bunch and I want them off the streets a.s.a.p.'

Ramsey nodded and stood up.

'Bloody ghosts,' snorted Blizzard, shaking his head as he watched the detective inspector head out into the corridor, a slight spring into his step. 'What do you make of it, David?'

'He is pretty worked up about it,' said Colley. 'Reckons you're not taking it seriously enough.'

Blizzard looked at him for a moment or two. It was well known among the officers at Abbey Road that few people could challenge the chief inspector's judgement but David Colley was one of them. With someone else there might have been an explosion from Blizzard at such impertinence from a junior officer but not with Colley.

'Maybe,' grunted Blizzard grudgingly, reaching for his mug of tea and tutting when he realized it had gone cold. 'Never get a chance to drink the blasted thing these days. So, apart from telling me I'm a silly old fool, what have you got on?'

'Nasty one,' said the sergeant. 'The headteacher at Heston Comp was assaulted outside the school gates on Friday night. Thought about it over the weekend and rang it in this morning.'

'That's whatsisname Howatch, isn't it?' asked Blizzard, looking at the sergeant with interest. 'The one with the sticky-up hair?'

'The very same,' grinned Colley.

'So assuming it wasn't an irate student from the hairdressing course, why would someone want to thump him?'

'Says it was kids flogging drugs.'

'Heston druggies again, eh?' murmured Blizzard with a gleam in his eye, adding mischievously, 'Maybe Chris can get his dark avenger to investigate it since we're short-staffed.'

'I'll let you tell him.'

'Maybe not,' smiled Blizzard. 'Somehow I don't think his sense of humour is up to it at the moment.'

'What sense of humour?' asked Colley innocently.

'Thank you for your input, Sergeant,' said Blizzard. 'Now, sod off and solve some crimes.'

Grinning, Colley hauled his tall frame out of the chair and ambled out into the corridor.

'And shut the door behind you!' shouted Blizzard. 'It's been like Piccadilly Circus in here this morning.'

The door slammed shut, leaving Blizzard alone with his thoughts. Ghost or no ghost, he reflected, drug dealing outside a school in a well-to-do place like Heston was bad news – and Blizzard knew it could only mean trouble.

CHAPTER **TWO**

The knock on Blizzard's office door just after two-thirty that afternoon came as a welcome relief for the chief inspector, who had experienced the kind of day he dreaded, tied up with seemingly endless paperwork. Give me villains any day, he thought morosely as he worked his way through the pile. It was his fault; he had deliberately ignored the growing mound of reports on his desk until he could do so no longer – it was beginning to block the light out – and had finally set aside Monday to deal with the backlog.

There were reports from the chief constable, reports from the deputy chief constable, reports from the assistant chief constable, reports from the Human Resources department (they went straight into the bin, life was too short for H R, reasoned Blizzard), several Home Office circulars and a number of items from community consultative forums. All very important, the chief inspector tried to tell himself, but paperwork was one of the things he hated about his job and, throughout the day, he had paused many times to stare out of the window and wish he was out on the street doing what he did best.

Looking up when he heard the knock, he groaned as the door swung open to reveal the bulky frame of Detective Chief Superintendent Arthur Ronald.

'If you've come to talk to me about the armed robbers again, you can naff off,' said Blizzard curtly.

'Good to see you showing respect for your senior officer,'

said Ronald with a twinkle in his eye, nodding approvingly at the pile of paperwork in the out tray. 'And that you are sorting that little lot out.'

'Under protest.'

Ronald noticed a pile of documents in the wastepaper basket.

'I hope that's not H R stuff,' he said suspiciously.

'Would I do a thing like that?' asked Blizzard innocently.

'You may not like it, but H R is....'

'Stuff H R,' said Blizzard. 'Anyway, did you come in for a fascinating chat on administration theory or was there something useful?'

'Actually,' said Ronald, smiling at the chief inspector's irritation, 'I wanted to talk about ghosts and ghoulies.'

'So, about this administration theory,' said Blizzard and gestured to the super to sit down.

'You don't get away with it that easily,' replied Ronald, sitting down heavily in the chair. 'We have got to get this ghost business sorted.'

'I know,' sighed Blizzard. 'I know.'

He and Ronald went back many years, having first worked together as rookie uniform officers, then in CID, before their careers went different ways. Blizzard had remained a detective but Ronald donned the blue and rose rapidly through the ranks. They had eventually been reunited at Abbey Road four years ago as Ronald returned, gratefully, to his CID roots to assume overall command of the southern half of the county.

They were very different characters. University-educated Ronald, married with two teenaged children, was a slightly pudgy, balding man with ruddy cheeks and eyes with bags sagging underneath them. A man given to constant worrying about mortgages and university fees, he was not yet fifty but looked older. A smart dresser with a sharply-pressed suit, tie always done up and shoes shined, he was a charming man with an easy manner and a gift for the kind of diplomacy that Blizzard had never possessed.

It was a gift that Ronald often needed in his job. Indeed, much of his time was spent covering for his outspoken colleague's outbursts. Ordinarily he would have begrudged the task but he held Blizzard in such high regard, personally and professionally, that he viewed it as a necessary part of his job. Blizzard respected him for that; underneath Ronald's affable exterior the chief inspector knew there lay a tough police officer and an extremely good detective. And that meant everything to Blizzard, who believed respect had to be earned rather than given of right. Not a view that made him popular among the pips in the corridors of power.

Blizzard was a markedly different character to his friend, the most obvious difference being in their attire. Aged in his mid-forties, Blizzard was dressed in his customary dark, slightly crumpled suit with tie dangling loosely, brown hair tousled as usual and with slight bags under clear blue eyes now tired with all the reading he had done that day.

But it was deeper than the way they dressed. No university for Blizzard, he had gone into the service straight from school and loved his job – paperwork allowing. Divorced for a number of years now, colleagues said he was really wedded to the job. He had usually worked in Hafton, virtually all of it plain-clothes, and had been promoted to take charge of Western Division CID as one of Ronald's first decisions after his appointment. Before Blizzard was given the job, the super had been forced to fight opposition from some of the top brass who resented the chief inspector's unwillingness to play the political game. John Blizzard did not care what they thought. He had no time for jargon or buzz words and told it like it was. Life, he often said, was too short to waste on misunderstandings. Some of the more fragile and less talented senior officers found the attitude threatening but although Ronald feigned exasperation at Blizzard's ways, if the truth be told, the chief inspector said the things that the super did not dare utter and Ronald quite enjoyed seeing the expressions on some of his colleagues' faces when they angrily recounted the conversations. And although he was a consummate player of the game and never said anything to suggest he agreed with his chief inspector, Ronald nevertheless managed to leave his colleagues in no doubt over where he stood. It was something to do with the fact that his mouth smiled sympathetically but his eyes never did.

If some senior officers found Blizzard's ways irksome, they endeared him to the hard-pressed detectives who worked out of Abbey Road. The police station had been the division's home since the late-1960s when it was constructed, supposedly as a temporary measure needed to take account of the rapidly expanding western area of Hafton. Three decades later it was still there, the green paint on the prefabs peeling, the windows grimy and the roof leaking. Successive chief constables had promised to replace it but something always went wrong and each passing year saw the ageing heating system clanking more loudly and break down more often and the maintenance team spending more time on repairs.

Although officers constantly complained about the station, they had limited time to notice its shortcomings because of the constant demands the division placed on them. Western covered a large area of the city, and one defined by sharp contrasts. On its western outskirts, just before the farming flatlands began, were the plush suburbs with their gravel drives, huge houses and outdoor swimming pools, owned by high-flying business people and the occasional villain who hid behind the respectable façade of pin-stripe suit and briefcase. Blizzard always used to say the houses had such big utility rooms because so much money was laundered there. He once got into a lot of trouble when he said it at a meeting with some senior officials from the city council. Arthur Ronald really earned his corn the day the official complaint was lodged.

Heading in towards the city centre, was the seamier side

of the division, run-down council estates with shuttered corner shops, abandoned pushchairs and burnt-out cars, neglected Victorian terraces owned by seedy landlords who had turned them into bedsit-land, and 1970s maisonette blocks stalked by heroin dealers and their addicts, places where police officers always went in pairs and where the few remaining respectable residents lived with those uneasy bedfellows, defiance and fear.

'What about ghosts?' asked Blizzard, tipping back on his chair.

Ronald took the evening newspaper out of his jacket pocket and tossed it on to the desk. Blizzard scowled as he surveyed the front page with a lurid artist's impression of the leering stranger beneath the screaming headline 'The Vengeance Man'.

'Marvellous,' sighed the chief inspector. 'I said it would be a bloody circus.'

'Circus or not, what are we doing about it, John?'

'I've got Chris looking at it but he's got plenty of other things on his plate. These robberies you keep going on about endlessly for a start.'

'I appreciate that,' nodded Ronald, not rising to the bait, 'but I want to make sure we are following up this Vengeance Man stuff as well.'

'Well we are,' nodded Blizzard. 'but there's a lot of people will not appreciate us chasing ghosts round grave-yards like something out of Benny Hill when our burglary rate is up five per cent this month and their corner shops keep getting done over.'

'Nevertheless, we need to be seen to be doing some-thing.'

'I know,' said Blizzard, tipping forward on his chair and hurling the newspaper at the bin, cursing as he missed. 'We do need to find this nutter. I don't want him giving other people ideas.'

'Well just as long as we are doing something,' said Ronald, heaving himself out of the chair. 'What with this attack on Mervyn Howatch at the school, the last thing we need is people thinking we are sitting on our hands. And it's not as if it's the first complaint we have had about drugs in the village is it?'

'No,' admitted Blizzard, adding slyly as the super headed for the door, 'In fact, if you like I could leave all this H R claptrap for another day and....'

Ronald's sour look said it all.

'Just an idea,' grinned Blizzard, picking up another report as the super headed out into the corridor.

The smile quickly fading as Blizzard thoughtfully watched his boss go. The chief inspector knew what was bugging Ronald. It was bugging him as well. There was nothing like crime in a well-to-do area to set the alarm bells ringing with the top brass. If someone was mugged on a seedy housing estate no one complained to the chief constable. If it happened in a posh street, you could guarantee he would get a call from one of his golfing buddies.

Heston had plenty of worthies, which is why Blizzard had listened to Colley's account of the assault on the head-teacher with concern. And why, despite his jokes at Ramsey's expense, he had also listened intently to the tales of the stranger in the graveyard. Not that he had given the DI that impression; Blizzard knew the damage to his credibility among the troops if he was seen to be taking ghost stories seriously. Now, thanks to the newspaper coverage, that all had to change. Time to focus on Heston.

Heston was once a fishing village, reliant on the brave men who sailed from its harbour into the river and out to the far-flung waters around Iceland and Greenland. A tight-knit, fiercely independent community, it had finally buckled under the dictats of Eurocrats in the seventies, most of the fleet having fallen victim to quotas and European politics. One or two fishermen continued to ply their trade but most of the vessels in the harbour now were pleasure boats, taking people on trips along the river or heading a little further out, making the short journey to the sea, laden with anglers or tourists eager to see the area's famous seal colony on the islands a mile or so off the estuary.

A proud and simple community once used to sorting out its own problems – the trawler men had fought their own battles, cleaned up their own wounded and refused to talk to the police – Heston had found that such an approach could not defeat Madame Progress. The village had fallen victim to the ever-growing conurbation of Hafton, which had encircled it on three sides with constantly encroaching housing estates. The centrally-heated little boxes were populated by upwardly mobile people who brought different attitudes to those held by the fishing folk. They were middle-class people who valued Heston's fishing industry only because it meant they could hang nice sepia pictures of grizzled old trawler men on their living room walls and wax lyrical about them at dinner parties. The few old-timers still living in Heston said they had killed off community spirit. People did not talk to each other any more, they said. And as the old-timers died, so did their way of life.

Behind its forced gentility – for all the mock Tudor timbers and replica Georgian houses, Heston could not do genuine gentility – there was another side to the village, as people insisted on still calling it. Drugs had arrived some years before but in those days there were only a few hard-core heroin users and police had always managed to keep them under control. However, that had changed and over recent months there had been reports of dramatically increased levels of heroin abuse in Heston, leading to several public meetings and complaints from everyone from the vicar to local councillors. In a funny way, mused Blizzard, the arrival of narcotics had created a community spirit where there had not been one for many years.

Because the drug dealing had been relatively low level, it had not really been an issue for Blizzard – he had been tying up loose ends on a couple of complicated murder inquiries anyway – and he had been happy to leave it to Chris Ramsey and his team. Now, with things having taken a more serious turn, and the headteacher reporting the blatant selling of drugs at the school gates, Blizzard was acutely aware that something had to be done to address the problem, and done quickly.

Such thoughts crowded in on him as he tried to concentrate on a rambling Home Office circular and found himself pausing more than once to stare out of the window at the gloomy winter sky. The thought that was occupying his mind was the ghostly figure in the graveyard. For all he had initially treated the appearance of the dark avenger as light relief, the news about the attack on the headteacher had imbued the events in the cemetery with a more serious import.

Indeed, throughout his lonely day climbing Mount Paperwork, the chief inspector's views had been changing and crystallizing. What if, he asked himself, the avenger was a sign that the community was losing faith in the police's ability to tackle the drug dealers? What if he represented the community's determination to take the law into its own hands? What if he was not actually a prankster but a vigilante? And even if he was a joker, what effect would his actions have? Talk of vigilantes was never a laughing matter. Rebuking himself for dismissing the incidents too lightly, Blizzard determined to talk to Chris Ramsey about it again. He did not relish having to eat humble pie before the detective inspector but it had to be done. He was always telling colleagues to admit to mistakes when they made them; now was the time to abide by his own mantra, he thought without much enthusiasm.

'Me and my big mouth,' he muttered, staring out of the window again.

Just after four, there was another knock on the door.

'Seen the paper?' asked Colley, walking in and waving the front page.

'Yes, thanks,' snorted Blizzard. 'Tabloid garbage!'

'I'm always impressed by the way you foster relation-ships with the media,' said Colley.

'You,' said Blizzard, jabbing his Biro at the sergeant, 'are beginning to sound like Arthur Ronald. Sit down.'

Grinning, the sergeant slumped in a chair and the chief inspector eyed him affectionately. Blizzard did not like many people but he liked David Colley. He found him approachable and friendly in a way that he did not experi-ence with the more uptight Chris Ramsey. Today, as always, the sergeant's black hair was neatly combed, his round, almost boyish face showed no signs of stubble, and his black trousers, blue shirt and grey jacket had all been perfectly ironed by Jay, his girlfriend. His shoes shone as usual. What was it about officers' shoes these days, thought Blizzard, covertly glancing down at his scuffed footwear?

Colley chuckled when he saw the movement and Blizzard cursed silently when he realized he had been rumbled. He always did when it happened but in reality he was not that bothered. There was an easy rapport between the two men. Aged in his mid-thirties, Colley had found himself increasingly assisting Blizzard with major inquiries over the past three years, usually at the DCI's request, and the chief inspector confided more in the sergeant than just about anyone, except perhaps the super. Their close rela-tionship was no secret in the police station, nor was it that Blizzard had earmarked Colley for Chris Ramsey's job when the DI moved on. It was a situation that irked Ramsey more and more.

'How's the DI?' asked Blizzard. 'Haven't seen him all day.'

'He's keeping out of your way. I told you this morning, you've upset him. He thinks you should be taking this churchyard business more seriously.'

'Maybe he's right,' nodded Blizzard, tossing a couple of reports into a bin already stuffed with paper.

'Aren't you supposed to file them or something?' asked Colley curiously.

'They are filed. You are definitely beginning to sound like Arthur Ronald.'

'Sorry.'

'Anyway, I know I shouldn't have laughed at Chris like that. Besides, I am changing my mind a bit now. Maybe he does have a point. Is he in?'

'No, he went out to talk to that shopkeeper who was thumped with the shotgun during the robbery on Saturday. He's out of hospital now. Then the DI said to tell you he is off to his martial arts class. They've got a big tournament or something coming up.'

'Hah bloody so,' grunted Blizzard.

'Which is why I thought I'd update you about the school job.'

'Go on.'

'Like I said, it's a nasty one,' said the sergeant, flicking open his pocket book. 'The head looked really rattled. Have you met Mervyn Howatch?'

'Not to talk to. Saw him at a couple of conferences in city hall. Funny hair, that's all I remember.'

'Funny eyes as well.'

'What do you mean?'

'Not sure. Scared, I suppose.'

'Go on.'

'According to Howatch, two weeks ago four former pupils started selling drugs at the school gates. Apparently, he told the local uniforms but they don't seem to have done much about it. Anyway, on Friday afternoon, they were back again and the head went out and confronted them. One of them punched him a couple of times.'

'Badly hurt?'

'Bit of bruising, nothing serious, but it has really shaken his confidence.'

'I can imagine – did he give you names?'

Colley nodded and held up his notebook.

'Yeah, two of them were known to us already. According to the local beat bobby....'

'Who is?'

'Fearnley.'

'Not sure I know him.'

'You'll have seen him, lots of gel in his hair. Struts about like a peacock. Always preening himself. Looks a bit vacant. God knows how he was accepted into the force.'

'Nice to see you showing respect for esteemed colleagues,' muttered Blizzard.

'Well, he's a nancy boy, what do you expect me to say? Anyway, I asked Fearnley and he said these lads were seen selling drugs on the wasteground near the recreation centre not so long ago.'

'Well, duh, pardon me for being thick but isn't PC Nancy Boy supposed to lift them for things like that?' asked Blizzard acidly.

'You might think....'

'Bloody uniform,' snorted Blizzard. 'No wonder the dark avenger or whatever he's called is hacked off. So, pray why were none of these likely lads arrested by the good constable?'

'He said no one was prepared to give evidence against them,' shrugged Colley. 'Same old story, guv. They're bad lads. Folks are scared.'

'Since when did that stop us feeling some collars?' replied Blizzard curtly.

'Yeah, but in his defence, sometimes....'

'Sometimes nothing,' said Blizzard firmly and scowled. 'Just because no one will talk shouldn't stop us nabbing people. Got to turn the pressure up on these people. Can't let them think they are above the law. You know that, David. It's as much about public reassurance as anything.'

'Now who's sounding like Arthur Ronald?'

'Actually, he sounds like me,' said Blizzard with a sardonic smile. 'Anyway, whichever way you look at it, it seems like uniform have slipped up on this one.'

'Certainly looks like it.'

'And,' said Blizzard briskly, sweeping up the unread

reports and dumping them in his now overflowing bin, 'we need to get this back under control p.d.q. Time to get back to some proper police work instead of all this garbage. I want those lads arrested.'

'That's the thing,' said Colley. 'They seem to have vanished into thin air.'

'A lot of people seem to do that in Heston,' grunted Blizzard. 'Well, they've got to be somewhere and I want you to get out there and find them. And if the DI kicks up a fuss about it tell him I ordered you to do it when he was out at origami or whatever he does.'

'Tai kwon do,' grinned the sergeant, heading out of the office, relieved that the chief inspector had at last switched out of paperwork mode into the energetic and decisive man he recognized.

After the sergeant had left, the late afternoon gloom descended on the office once more. Darkness was falling and, disturbed by what he had heard, Blizzard stared out of the rain-flecked window at the grey sky. It would soon be the Vengeance Man's time again, he thought with a sense of foreboding. Something was happening in Heston that he did not fully understand and despite himself, he felt a shiver run down his spine.

CHAPTER **THREE**

All thoughts of the unearthly goings-on in Heston graveyard were put to the back of everyone's minds later that week by something very much of this world. Normally, Blizzard would have welcomed something to divert attention from the ghost. Since the local paper had run its front page article, the national media, as the chief inspector had feared, had seized on the story and Heston had become the subject of much interest from reporters, including several film crews, even one from a Japanese television station whose over-enthusiastic reporter had bounced excitedly around the village green, jabbering away ten to the dozen. And a local paranormal society had tried to stage an event in the churchyard before the exasperated vicar called the police and they abandoned the plan.

Throughout all of this, Blizzard had curtly refused all requests from the press office to give an interview. He might ordinarily have allowed Ramsey to talk to the press but the DI had been off two days caring for his young daughter, who was ill and off school and whose mother was away on a course. When he had heard about the enforced absence, Blizzard had been frustrated – there were serious crimes to be tackled – but he accepted it without comment. This was not the time to muddy the waters with his DI. Their chat about the ghost would have to wait.

The result of all this was that a grumbling Detective Chief Superintendent Arthur Ronald had been forced to answer the media's questions about the Vengeance Man, much against his better judgement. And very silly he sounded, too, thought Blizzard cheerfully, as he watched his boss on early evening local television news trying to put a serious spin on the story. For all that, the whole affair had lifted spirits in Abbey Road Police Station, something to be welcomed at a time when the force was experiencing the usual spike in crimes after the arrival of the dark nights. However, light-hearted story or not, the chief inspector regarded it as an unwanted distraction and had been driven to issue a stern warning to his CID officers that there were some real criminals to catch. Such was the tone of his voice that the gossip had stopped from that moment – at least it did when the detectives reckoned he might hear them.

As luck would have it, that Thursday, having spent the morning at a meeting at headquarters, Blizzard was back in his office shortly after three when the call came through that diverted attention back to the real world. For all Blizzard wanted minds concentrated, he would never have wanted it to be achieved in such a shocking and brutal fashion. Ramsey told him that a shopkeeper in a suburb of Heston had reported three suspicious men hanging around outside his store. The call set alarm bells ringing for the detectives, who had been increasingly concerned about the activities of the new gang of armed robbers operating in the city over recent weeks, with all but one of their offences committed in Western Division.

The first attack had been worrying enough with a masked man walking into a corner shop and pointing a gun at the terrified shopkeeper before stealing a couple of hundred pounds from the till. Since then there had been three more attacks, each one more violent than the last with the gang selecting ever-larger establishments in their quest for more money. The detectives had quickly ruled out a racist motive – something they considered because the first victim was a Pakistani – because the three subsequent attacks were all on white shopkeepers. Between them, they had netted the gang thousands of pounds and they showed no sign of stopping.

Two things worried Blizzard and his colleagues: they were new kids on the block and an unknown quantity and they were showing an alarming willingness to use violence on their victims. The latest attack, on the previous Saturday, had been the worst one, taking place at a branch of a well-known local chain-store not far from Abbey Road Police Station. The shopkeeper and five customers, including a mother and toddler, had been threatened with shotguns by three masked men. When the shopkeeper started to protest, he was knocked unconscious with the butt of the gun, a vicious assault that had seen him hospitalized and so traumatized that he was reluctant to give evidence to the police and was talking about quitting his job and leaving the area.

Although the threats had grown more violent with each robbery, it was the first time the gang had actually harmed anyone – and everyone knew that kind of escalation meant big trouble. More worrying was the fact that none of the usual police informants were saying much, their handlers, Ramsey and Colley included, gaining the distinct impression that people were genuinely terrified of the gang. In the detectives' experience, at least one informant would normally break ranks in cases like this but not this time – and that worried everyone at Abbey Road Police Station. A new crew on the manor, escalating levels of violence and silent informants meant bad news for everyone.

So when Ramsey rang through about the suspicious characters in Acacia Walk, part of the shopping area at the heart of a seventies estate on the edge of Heston, it was enough for Blizzard to throw his jacket on and head for the car park, where he was joined by a sprinting Colley. Ramsey was already on his way with a couple of uniforms in a marked car.

It took the two detectives just four minutes to reach the

open-air precinct and as Blizzard hurled his car round the corner, they saw that the marked patrol vehicle containing Ramsey and the uniformed officers was already blocking off the other end, a short distance from the shop, which was sandwiched between a carpet store and a chippy. Wailing sirens in the distance indicated that more officers were on the way, including members of the force's armed response team.

'We need these bastards before they kill someone,' muttered Blizzard, bringing the car to a halt less than 20 yards from the store.

All seemed quiet.

'What do you think?' asked Colley, surveying the scene with trepidation.

'Not sure yet.'

'Anything?' Ramsey's voice crackled over the radio from the patrol car at the other end of the street.

'No sign of anything,' said Blizzard, reaching for the car door handle. 'Let's go and take a look but I don't want any heroics. No....'

He had no chance to finish his comment because there was a loud shotgun blast from the store and the front door was hurled open with such ferocity that it was ripped from its hinges, sending glass showering across the pavement. Three masked men, all wielding sawn-off shotguns burst into the road just as their getaway car screeched round the corner behind Blizzard, slamming into the back of his vehicle and sending it careering across the road, before juddering to a halt outside the store.

By now, the masked men had spotted the police and one of them was pointing his shotgun at the marked patrol vehicle. An instant later there was a loud report and the front windscreen of the police car was shattered, a second shot bringing a jet of steam from the buckled bonnet, sending Ramsey and the uniformed officers tumbling out into the street and scuttling for cover. Cowering behind the car, they peered out to be met by a shot from one of the other robbers, which sailed above their heads and embedded itself into a tree.

'Bloody hell!' cried Blizzard, as he recovered from the collision and looked out to see the first gunman re-loading and slowly and deliberately turning his weapon in their direction.

Blizzard moved quicker than he had ever done before, throwing the car sharply into reverse and sending it squealing back down the road with smoke billowing from its tyres, but not fast enough to avoid the shot which smashed into the headlight. As the chief inspector battled to control his spinning car, the masked men leapt into the getaway vehicle, which roared the other way, one of the robbers leaning out as they grew closer to the patrol car and firing off another shot at the sheltering officers, the bullet missing and ploughing into the front door of a nearby house. Then it was away, weaving past an arriving patrol car, clipping its front end, and careering off through the estate, forcing the armed response vehicle to swerve into a bus-stop. Blizzard could hear the getaway car's engine protesting and the tyres screeching, the sound rapidly receding into the distance. It was all over in a few seconds.

'Jesus,' breathed the ashen-faced chief inspector, stumbling out of his car and looking in disbelief at the smashed headlight, before regaining his wits and reaching in for the radio and firing off instructions to control.

A shaken Colley had thrown himself from the vehicle and was running towards the store on legs that were still trembling. Inside, he found two terrified customers, an old lady and a young man, hiding behind some shelves. On the floor lay the writhing shopkeeper, blood pouring from an ugly leg wound, the colour rapidly draining from his face.

'Hang on, mate,' said Colley, whipping out his handkerchief to create a makeshift tourniquet. 'The ambulance is on its way.'

'I was giving them the money,' moaned the shopkeeper,

a white-haired man in his mid-fifties. 'I was giving them the money.'

'I know,' said Colley, wrapping the tourniquet round his leg.

Moments later, other officers had entered the store and were looking after the customers, and the ambulance crew had arrived. Blizzard watched them working rapidly on the injured shopkeeper and wandered over to examine the torn-off front door, which was dangling on a single hinge. He shook his head. This lot were scary. The chief inspector stood aside to let the ambulance men carry the injured man out.

'We have to get these psychos,' he said to Ramsey with a grim expression on his face as he watched the victim loaded into the ambulance. 'They're going to kill someone next time.'

'They might have done it this time,' said Colley, joining them. 'He didn't look too clever. You OK?'

Blizzard, still pale and shaky, nodded.

'Chris,' he said, placing a hand on the detective inspector's shoulder. 'Take as many officers as you need. If this lot get away, I want them found and locked up soon p.d.q. They are dangerous.'

'You're telling me,' said Ramsey, heart still racing as he recalled the sound of the bullet shattering the windscreen.

'Do you need to see the quack?' asked Blizzard, eyeing the blood seeping from a gash on the DI's cheek, caused by a flying shard of glass.

'No, no, I'm alright.'

'Good man. Go on then. Oh, and Chris, be careful – this lot don't mind killing poliss.'

'No need to tell me,' said the DI, adding hesitantly, 'Guv, I hate to bring this up at a time like this but what do I do about our loony in the graveyard? Press office rang me today to ask for an update.'

Blizzard considered his response carefully, unwilling to further damage the officer's confidence, particularly when he had just been shot at, and mindful of the pledge he had made to Ronald to address the strange happenings in Heston churchyard.

'He's got to be a low priority at the moment,' he said after a moment or two, 'but we do need to do something about him.'

He walked over to the DI and said quietly so that only Colley among the other officers could hear.

'I should have listened to you more seriously, Chris. My mistake. Let's see how we get on with this lot then get someone to take a look at the ghost. But I do want this joker nabbed. He's too much of a distraction and one we can ill afford to waste time on while these lunatics are running around playing cops and robbers.'

'Thank you,' nodded Ramsey, buoyed by the support.

'Not like you to admit your mistakes,' said Colley, sense of humour returning as Ramsey headed out of the door.

'It'll give him a boost. Besides, the Vengeance Man or whatever he calls himself is playing a dangerous game,' said Blizzard grimly. 'You don't muck about with drug dealers and I want him caught before he gets himself hurt....'

CHAPTER **FOUR**

'We needn't have worried about him being hurt, then,' said Colley flatly.

Blizzard made no reply. None was needed. The grisly sight in front of them was eloquent enough. It was one thirty on the following Monday morning and the detectives were standing in the chill darkness at the far side of Heston churchyard, near a low tumbledown wall beyond which, through a band of trees, they could just make out the football fields in the wan moonlight. Coats turned up against the driving rain and shivering in the biting cold, they gazed down grimly at the body of a young man, slumped over an overturned gravestone.

As the sergeant shone his torch on the teenager, he winced. You never really got used to death. The officers could clearly see illuminated in the beam the gaping wound in his head and the copious amounts of blood that had spilled down his face, still wet and glistening. Close by lay a large chunk of stone, once part of the gravestone but long since weathered and snapped off by decades of wind-lashed rain. The gravestone itself had been laid down several years before by order of the council, amid concerns that it could topple and kill a small child. Ironic really; it had ended up killing someone after all. The heavy bloodstaining and the clump of matted hair on the sheared-off chunk clearly revealed it to be the crude weapon used by the killer.

Colley, still struggling to recover his composure after

being fired at outside the shop a few days earlier, dragged his eyes away from the gruesome scene, glanced round and shivered. Apart from the pale moonlight, the darkness was also penetrated, if faintly, by the orange street lights several hundred feet away and the rhythmic blue flashing from the police vehicles parked at the main gates. The result was darting shadows everywhere and Colley tried to dispel from his mind the irrational thought that, beneath the boughs of the trees, over where the parish church loomed dimly above them, where the dark met the light, the gravestones seemed to grow in size and move. Adding to his foreboding was the silence, broken only by the soft sound of rain falling gently on the curled and brown dead winter leaves that carpeted the sodden ground.

'Spooky place,' said the sergeant instinctively before inwardly rebuking himself and concentrating on the job in hand.

Blizzard, who had seemed less affected by the shootings – although who could know what was going on behind his inscrutable features? – and who now seemed less moved by the eerie atmosphere, glanced round and nodded.

'Perfect place for a murder,' he said and gestured at the gravestones. 'Cuts out the middle man, see.'

They had been summoned shortly after one by a breathless Chris Ramsey, who had been called out by the Control Room following reports of the Vengeance Man by a drunken teenager wending his way home from a friend's house. Since the shooting in Heston, the Vengeance Man had been almost forgotten by the detectives of Western Division and even the media had lost interest, discouraged in part by the parish vicar's refusal to let them film there at night. With the police declining further requests for interview, the story had started to – as it were – die a death. Even the Japanese television reporter had gone off to bounce about somewhere else.

Besides, all CID efforts had been thrown into the search for the robbers following their high speed escape from

Heston in a cloud of squealing rubber. After the shooting, they had driven at speeds of up to 100mph as far as the eastern bypass, pursued by several patrol cars. Failing to take a bend, the getaway vehicle had slammed into a tree and the gang had run off across the fields, the gunman pausing for a moment or two to loose off a couple of shots at pursuing officers. The shots slammed into a couple of trees but the officers spoke later about the coolness with which he aimed at them, and how they felt fortunate to be alive to tell the tale. And with each telling and re-telling of the story for wide-eyed audiences of young constables, the shots got closer and the danger grew greater. Only the grizzled old sergeants were not impressed; they had seen too much in their long years in the force.

Despite the efforts of the force helicopter and a massive door-to-door search by officers, the gang melted into the nearby housing estate and had not been seen since. Reporting directly to Arthur Ronald, Blizzard and Ramsey had found themselves far too busy chasing up lines of inquiry and organizing their detectives to worry about the Vengeance Man until the early morning phone call from control, which said the drunken teenager had seen the stranger loping down Heston High Street.

Ramsey had hurriedly thrown on some clothes and within a few minutes was sitting talking to the young boy at the local police station. The stranger, said the boy, had been striding down the high street towards him, neither looking left or right. The boy had hidden behind a phone box and saw the Vengeance Man stop when he spied a local drug user trying to break into a car on the edge of the market place, seeking something to sell to feed his habit. Since drugs had arrived in the village, car crime had gone steadily upwards. Intent on his work, and not seeing the stranger until he was almost upon him, the teenager had whirled round, screamed and fled for dear life. The Vengeance Man seemed then to have disappeared into the night.

Ramsey had not expected to find much when he arrived

in Heston. Since the publicity surrounding the case, the force had received a number of hoax calls but he was quickly convinced by the boy's account, which was then confirmed by a woman walking her dog. She called in at the station to report what she had seen. An increasingly uneasy Ramsey had ordered a search of the area and he and a couple of PCs had summoned up their courage and headed for the graveyard, which was when they stumbled across the body.

One of the constables had apprehended a teenage drug taker, whom he found cowering behind a tree at the gates and who had blurted out to the DI that he had also seen the Vengeance Man. The teenager said he had been at the graveyard to buy heroin from his regular dealer. Having purchased his drugs, the young man had scuttled from the churchyard only to hear his dealer cry out seconds later. Turning back at the gates, he had been horrified to see the Vengeance Man rushing towards him – almost floating above the gravestones, he had told Ramsey with a shudder.

The boy had hurled himself behind a tree and watched in terror as the Vengeance Man turned to stare at him – the teenager started to tremble at this point – then strode on to the road and away. The boy had not dared venture out of his hiding place until the police arrived and found him, still whimpering behind the tree and terrified half to death. Listening to his story, only recounted after several minutes of coaxing, Ramsey had felt the goosebumps rising. Now, having left the teenager with a constable and completed a cursory search of the rest of the graveyard, Ramsey was heading back to the murder scene.

'Anything?' asked Blizzard grimly as the DI's torchlight picked its way through the gravestones, acutely aware that his jokes of previous weeks had suddenly fallen very flat indeed.

'Nothing,' replied Ramsey, throwing his arms out wide. 'He's vanished into thin air.'

'Don't start that malarkey again,' snapped the chief inspector. 'People don't just disappear. He must have gone somewhere.'

Despite the angry exclamation, Chris Ramsey allowed himself a small smile. At last, he thought, the chief inspector was taking the Vengeance Man seriously.

'What are you grinning at?' demanded Blizzard.

'Nothing, sir,' said Ramsey.

'I know what you're thinking,' said Blizzard, flash of temper banished as quickly as it had erupted. 'Well, I'm taking this loony seriously now, all right? Where's the kid who saw him?'

'Over by the gates – won't come in.'

'I don't blame him,' said Colley instinctively.

'Don't you start,' muttered Blizzard. 'It's only a sodding graveyard. They're all dead anyway.'

'That's what worries me,' said Colley as the officers walked back across the graveyard by torchlight, picking their way tentatively through the overgrown grass, the sergeant yelling out in pain as he cracked his shin on a headstone concealed by years of vegetation growth. At the gates, the nervous teenager was standing with a constable who seemed just as uneasy and kept glancing anxiously towards the churchyard. Blizzard eyed the teenager dubiously; the boy had that thin, sallow, bloodless look of a heroin addict, and was surveying them with frightened, darting eyes. His black windcheater and jeans were covered in mud where had slipped while fleeing the killer and one of his hands was bleeding where he had smashed it into the tree in his desperation to find a hiding place.

Blizzard said thinly, 'You look like you've seen a ghost.'

'It ain't funny!' exclaimed the boy.

'It certainly isn't. What's your name?'

'Billy Thompson.'

'And how old are you?'

'Sixteen.'

'Still at school?'

'Just left Heston Comp.'

Colley and Blizzard exchanged glances. The school seemed to be cropping up throughout all their inquiries.

'So this thing,' asked Blizzard. 'What did you see of him?'

'It were awful,' and the boy shuddered. 'He were huge, must have been six foot, and he seemed to float above the ground, like.'

'This isn't Ghostbusters,' sighed Blizzard. 'Just stick to the truth. Did you see him attack your mate?'

'Na, but I heard it,' and Thompson closed his eyes, shuddering as he recalled the scene. 'Heard him scream. It were terrible. And he ain't my mate. I just buy me drugs off him. How is he anyway?'

'He's dead,' said Blizzard bluntly.

'Oh, God,' whispered the young man, staggering slightly and having to be supported by the uniform constable. 'I fought he was just given a good howking.'

'As good as they get,' said Blizzard, sensing that the boy's shock was a genuine reaction.

Nevertheless, Thompson was, as it stood, someone who still had to be eradicated from their inquiries before they could move on.

'Then the killer came for you?' asked the chief inspector after giving the teenager time to compose himself.

This time only a dumb nod from the boy, the memory too raw and terrible to allow words. Thompson looked down at the ground and did not speak for a moment or two.

'How come he didn't attack you?' asked Blizzard.

Something in his voice made the teenager look up. Angrily. He shrugged off the uniform constable's hold.

'This ain't nothing to do with me!' he exclaimed.

'So how come he didn't attack you as well?' repeated Blizzard. 'It's a simple question.'

'I dived behind a tree,' and the boy began to sob.

Again, they seemed genuine tears, thought the chief inspector.

'Did he say anything to you?' asked Colley, taking over the questioning, hoping that his less harsh approach might elicit some more information from the cowed teenager.

'Yeah,' nodded Thompson. 'He said "tell the others".'

'Others?'

'I don't know who he meant, honest.'

'Tell them what?'

'Dunno.'

'Picked the wrong person to leave the message with really, didn't he?' murmured Blizzard thinly.

Colley chuckled.

'Are you going to give us the name of your dealer, Billy?' asked Ramsey.

The teenager hesitated.

'Na,' he said at length.

'Come on, Billy,' remonstrated Ramsey but the teenager shook his head vigorously.

'For God's sake, Billy,' exclaimed Blizzard in exasperation. 'He's dead – he can't hurt you now.'

'But his mates can,' replied Thompson, shooting nervous glances around him, almost as if he expected them to leap out from behind the trees.

'The name, Billy!'

This time the question from Blizzard was asked with a harsh, almost threatening, edge in his voice. The teenager eyed the stern-faced chief inspector for a moment, realizing that the detective was just as scary as the dealers.

'Alright,' he mumbled. 'Eddie Barton.'

Colley gave a low whistle.

'You know him?' asked Blizzard.

'I'm getting to,' nodded the sergeant. 'Nasty piece of work.'

And he lowered his voice.

'Barton,' he said, 'is one of the kids who was confronted by the headteacher over at Heston Comp. In fact, Mervyn Howatch said he was the one who hit him. He's one of the lads we've been looking for.'

'Well,' said Blizzard sardonically as he gestured back into the graveyard, 'looks like you've found him.'

He watched grim-faced as the forensics team picked its way through the headstones.

'I was beginning to think that this was all an elaborate hoax,' he said. 'That maybe this Vengeance Man character did not even exist. Maybe someone just wanted to waste our time when we were supposed to be investigating the robberies. Or maybe that it was a loony.'

'The idea occurred to me as well,' nodded Ramsey. 'Particularly with all those crank calls we have been getting. But now this....'

His voice tailed off.

'Indeed,' murmured Blizzard. 'But now this....'

CHAPTER **FIVE**

Now everything had changed. Ghouls cavorting round graveyards was one thing, cold-blooded murder was another, so it was that early next morning, and after a few snatched and troubled hours of sleep, Blizzard was ensconced in Ronald's office at Abbey Road, discussing the events of the night before. Shortly after nine, with the officers deep in conversation across the desk, there was a knock on the door and Colley walked in.

'I may have got a suspect for you,' announced the sergeant.

'And after lunch you'll be arresting Lord Lucan, I suppose,' said the chief inspector drily.

'Who, pray, is this suspect?' asked Ronald eagerly, leaning forward, mindful that a quick clear-up always went down well with the chief constable.

His delight did not last long.

'Mervyn Howatch,' announced Colley proudly.

'Who?' asked the superintendent.

'The headteacher of Heston Comp,' explained Blizzard, enjoying the superintendent's crestfallen expression despite his own disappointment. 'The one with the funny sticky-up hair.'

'But he's as respectable as they come,' moaned Ronald. 'Why don't you arrest the Pope while you're at it?'

'The Pontiff has got a good alibi,' said Colley, straight-faced. 'Sundays are quite busy for Popes, apparently.'

Blizzard chuckled. His sergeant's irreverent, often light-hearted, approach to life had always appealed to him, which was why he preferred Colley to the more serious-minded Chris Ramsey.

'So how come you want to clap our Mr Howatch in irons?' asked Ronald gloomily. 'I don't recall anyone announcing that murder was on the National Curriculum.'

'The school has just rung up. According to Mr Howatch's wife, he went out in the car about seven last night – said he was off to visit his elderly mother in a home on the east side. Hasn't been seen since.'

'Go on,' said Ronald, interest well and truly engaged.

'Well, don't you think that it's a bit of a coincidence that our smack man Eddie Barton ends up with his head cream-crackered on the same night the guy he dunched does a runner?'

'Does your sergeant speak English?' asked Ronald sourly, grimacing at the use of slang.

'Sometimes,' said Blizzard, getting to his feet. 'Come on, Sergeant, I think it is time we went back to school.'

'Careful, John,' warned Ronald as they headed out of his office. 'Folks are upset enough about what's been happening in Heston without you stirring things up even more. They already think we've failed them by not stamping on the drug dealing earlier....'

'And they'd be right.'

Blizzard's cool gaze dared his superior officer to challenge the statement. Ronald did not rise to the challenge. He knew the chief inspector was right.

'Whatever,' said Ronald guardedly. 'All I'm saying is that the last thing we need is you accusing their head-teacher of being Zorro or whatever this character is called.'

'You know me,' said Blizzard, turning at the door and beaming at the superintendent.'

'Yes, I do,' sighed Ronald. 'That's why I said it.'

He could hear Blizzard chuckling long after he had left the room.

CHAPTER **SIX**

Blizzard did not like schools. Correction. He did not like teenagers and they spent a lot of their time in schools so he didn't like schools. He did not like teachers either; all those holidays (he made an exception for Colley's live-in girlfriend Jay, a primary school teacher of whom Blizzard was very fond). But most of all, he did not like the Sixth Form Common Room at Heston Comprehensive, populated as it was with bored-looking teenagers lounging about on sofas, chatting idly, making calls on their mobile telephones and chewing gum. The pupils eyed the officers without much interest.

'Too little respect these days,' grunted Blizzard as he was forced to step over the outstretched legs of a teenager.

'What do you expect them to do, stand up and salute?' asked Colley mischievously.

'They should know better,' grunted the chief inspector, whose mood had been worsened by lack of sleep.

'Of course they should,' said Colley soothingly.

He had heard it all before from his chief inspector, who, mid-forties going on mid-nineties was becoming increasingly intolerant in his old age and, never having had children during his failed marriage, did not have a particularly strong empathy with young people. It was also, Colley reflected, one of the downsides of being a copper that you tended to base your view on life on the people you met – and most of the young people he and Blizzard met during the course of their jobs were in some kind of trouble. Much of the chief inspector's prejudices had been reaffirmed, recalled the sergeant, by two teenagers three years before. They had been carrying out distraction burglaries in the Western Division, one keeping the old dear talking on the front doorstep while the other slipped in through the back door and rifled through her valuables. The crimes had devastated their victims and cost one her life. When she discovered that her life savings were missing, she had suffered a massive heart attack and died before the ambulance got her to hospital. When they were arrested, the teenagers, who were only fourteen, had shown such a lack of compassion for the pensioner and such a lack of respect for the police that it had shocked even the hardened detectives. Adding to the chief inspector's irritation was that the CPS refused to bring a manslaughter charge. The boys got off with a paltry fine for a minor offence. Blizzard had talked about the incident for weeks afterwards.

Now, the chief inspector led the way across the room, ignoring the hostile looks from those students who had worked out pretty rapidly that they were police officers. Which was just about all of them. The detectives had arrived at the school's front reception a few minutes before and asked for John Pendrie, the deputy headteacher, who was, the bespectacled receptionist had said with an airy waft of a manicured hand, in the common room. Blizzard walked towards the coffee bar at the far end of the room, his nose wrinkling at the stifling fug of acrid cigarette smoke. Colley was pretty sure he also detected the aroma of cannabis as well but that could wait. They had bigger problems to confront.

'What happened to healthy living?' grunted Blizzard sourly, wafting the smoke away.

'Talking of healthy living, as I recall you had two bacon sandwiches for breakfast,' said Colley mischievously. 'I don't know, all that grease....'

'I have to be careful,' grunted Blizzard. 'If a vitamin were to get into my bloodstream who knows what damage it could do. Besides, smoking is different.'

'Yes, but it's cool when you are their age,' explained Colley.

'Perhaps they think dying of lung cancer is cool as well,' muttered Blizzard. 'When I was at school....'

'Do go on,' said Colley with a wicked smile. 'I do so like to hear about life under Queen Victoria. What *were* the Peelers like, guv?'

'All I am saying,' said the chief inspector, pointedly ignoring the comment, 'is that schools are supposed to teach our young people respect for their elders.'

'God, you do sound like my mother,' grinned Colley.

Blizzard paused for a moment, considered the response then gave a wry smile before shaking his head again as he surveyed the students with their tattered jeans and T-shirts, raising an eyebrow at a couple of girls standing over by the window, with black hair, black eyes, black make-up and black clothing.

'What are they supposed to be going as?' he asked.

'Goths,' explained Colley.

'Why aren't they in uniform?'

'Sixth formers don't have to wear it. It's part of their right to self-expression, apparently.'

Blizzard snorted and, feeling uncomfortably out of place, approached the coffee bar counter, next to which lounged a bored-looking teenager in a black T-shirt, on the front of which was emblazoned the word Death and a grinning skull with snakes slithering from the eye sockets.

The boy looked the besuited detectives up and down slowly then drawled, 'Don't tell me, you're from the fashion police.'

Blizzard glared at him and Colley struggled to contain a smile. The boy noticed the younger man's reaction and grinned.

'We're looking for your deputy headteacher,' said Blizzard curtly.

'John's in the office.'

'Well can you tell *Mister* Pendrie that we are here,' growled the chief inspector.

'Just go through,' and the student gestured to a side door.

Glowering even more, Blizzard entered the office to see a man in his late forties, maybe even touching fifty, reading from some notes on the cluttered desk. Dressed in brown cords, a brown cord jacket and a green shirt with a yellow tie, John Pendrie was six feet tall, his frame wiry and spare, his face lean but slightly lined, the hair brown but thinning on top.

'Can I help you, gentlemen?' he asked in a slightly nasal voice.

'I'm Chief Inspector Blizzard, this is Sergeant Colley.'

'You're here about our Mr Howatch, I imagine,' said Pendrie, gesturing to Colley. 'Well, I told your officer here all I know about the attack the last time he was here.'

'Indeed,' nodded Blizzard, sitting down. 'But I want to hear what happened again.'

'I can't tell you much,' shrugged Pendrie. 'I went early because of a dentist's appointment that day. From what I can gather, Mervyn confronted a gang of ex-students who had been selling drugs outside the gate.'

'Had they been doing it for long?' asked Colley.

'Too long,' nodded Pendrie. 'We did ask the police to do something about it but nothing happened. Apparently they had been selling the stuff on the waste ground then they started selling to kids through a hole in the fence at lunchtimes. When we repaired the fence, they started selling at the front gates.'

'How did Mr Howatch take that?'

'Badly,' and Pendrie leaned forward conspiratorially. 'He's a worrier is our Mervyn. Took it very personally.'

'You can see why,' replied Blizzard ascerbically. 'After

all, you are supposed to be teaching them the right way to live, aren't you? The last thing you want is them taking drugs, surely.'

'Yes, but there has to be an element of self-determination,' said Pendrie. 'We teach them the facts but they must make up their own minds. The just say no approach only alienates them.'

'Whatever,' grunted an unimpressed Blizzard. 'Tell me what happened when Mr Howatch was attacked.'

'From what I hear, he appealed to their better natures, to their sense of loyalty to the school badge,' and Pendrie laughed drily. 'Very Mervyn that.'

The detectives exchanged glances; something in the tone of voice suggested a deep lack of respect for his colleague and, in particular, it grated on Blizzard, who was already irritated by the attitude shown by his students.

'And is that when Barton hit him?' asked the chief inspector, struggling to remain civil.

'Yes.'

'Another example of self-determination, I imagine,' said Blizzard coldly.

'No, it was wrong.'

Pendrie met the angry chief inspector's look with commendable calmness. He knew what the police officers were thinking.

'Presumably you knew Eddie Barton?' asked Colley, deciding that a row between his chief inspector and the teacher would not benefit anyone.

'Oh, yes, everyone knew Eddie Barton,' and Pendrie shook his head sadly. 'Nasty piece of work he was by the end.'

'The end?'

'Yes, he was a nice enough kid when he arrived, bit quiet, in fact. I think there had been problems at home. I thought he might be OK but he started running with the wrong bunch. They bullied a lot of the smaller kids and

Eddie got himself expelled twice. The last time for striking a teacher. He was always going to get himself into serious trouble.'

'Well he's done it properly this time,' said Blizzard bluntly. 'Someone murdered him last night.'

Pendrie gave a low whistle.

'How?' he asked.

'Had his head stoved in in the graveyard.'

Pendrie nodded.

'They sold their drugs there as well apparently. So he's dead, is he? Can't say I'm surprised.'

'How did you know they were selling drugs in the graveyard?' asked Colley.

'You hear things as a teacher. We told all this to your local constable a few weeks ago, chap called Fearnley or something,'

'So why the hell didn't he do anything about it?' exclaimed an exasperated Blizzard, reminding himself to talk to the uniform inspector responsible for the officer's conduct.

'I don't know,' said Pendrie, walking over to the kettle. 'You're the policeman, Mr Blizzard. Tea?'

The detectives nodded.

'When I talked to Mervyn's wife this morning, she told me that he was more worried than usual,' said Colley. 'Was that true?'

'Difficult to imagine him being more worried than usual but yes,' said Pendrie, busying himself with making the tea, grimacing as he peered at the muck at the bottom of one of the mugs.

'Meaning?'

'He's a worrier, our Mervyn. There were a lot of pressures on him.'

'Such as?'

Pendrie turned round.

'There's some bad stuff going down,' he said earnestly, the first time he had appeared particularly concerned about the situation. 'Ofsted is due here in a week or two and Mervyn is convinced we will get a bad report. He's probably right. Our last exam results were abysmal and we have had one or two disciplinary problems.'

'Get away,' murmured the chief inspector.

Pendrie ignored the comment.

'Then there's the rumour that the council has us earmarked for closure.'

'Why?' asked Blizzard.

'Usual reason,' said Pendrie, handing over the tea, sitting down at the table and taking a sip. 'They need to save money and with our problems we're a sitting duck. Apparently it's between us and Forest Glades. Which one would you pick?'

The detectives nodded. Forest Glades (no forest, no glades), three miles away, was the best school in the city, always top of the league tables and attracting the very best pupils, many from the villages. Pendrie's school may have been in leafy, upwardly mobile Heston but its catchment stretched on to some of the rougher estates further towards the city centre and its academic record was nowhere near as good as Forest Glades.

'So when these lads started selling drugs, it was the final straw for the headteacher,' mused Blizzard. 'When did they leave Heston Comp?'

'Three years ago. They must all be nineteen now.'

'I've got the names of the others,' said Colley, referring to his notebook. 'Roger Colclough, Paul Moody and Raymond Ransome.'

'That's them,' nodded Pendrie. 'A bad lot.'

'And Mervyn was particularly upset at what they were doing?' asked Blizzard.

'Like I said, Mervyn is old school, Chief Inspector,' said Pendrie. 'Big believer in discipline, particularly when it comes to things like drugs.'

'Looking at the state of your common room, I'm tempted to agree,' murmured Blizzard.

'Kids need to be allowed some space,' replied Pendrie evenly.

'Yes, but not to be spaced out,' said Blizzard sardonically. 'And what about respect? What happened to that?'

'You sound like Mervyn but it does not work that way, Chief Inspector. He believed the kids would do whatever he said so when he found out that four former pupils were flogging heroin outside the front gate he took it really hard. It made it personal for him, like he had failed. Same with the bullying that goes on. He takes it as a personal slight against him. It's like he owns the kids that come here.'

'Surely that's the sign of a good professional,' said Blizzard.

'There's a limit to what you can do,' shrugged Pendrie.

'You could expel them.'

'We could, we did and we do but they've got to come back sometime. We tried palming one or two off to other schools – Eddie Barton and Roger Colcough were among them actually – but the schools kicked up a fuss and we got the little beggars back.'

'Mervyn's wife said he reckoned he was ill,' said Colley.

'He gets these headaches,' nodded Pendrie. 'He's convinced himself that he's got a brain tumour.'

'And has he?'

'Wouldn't have thought so,' shrugged Pendrie. 'But who knows? He refused to go to the doctor to have it checked out. Personally, my money's on stress.'

'I can see why,' said Blizzard, draining his cup and standing up, suddenly weary of Pendrie's complacent attitude.

'Don't judge this school, or me, too quickly, Chief Inspector,' said Pendrie, taking the clinking mugs to the sink. 'They're good kids. The likes of Eddie Barton and his mates are a small minority.'

'I'll have to take your word for that,' said the chief inspector and stalked out of the room.

'He'd get on well with our Mr Howatch,' said Pendrie to

Colley as they followed Blizzard out into the fug of the common room. 'He doesn't understand kids either.'

'Well self-expression or not,' said the sergeant, nodding at a group of students lounging in the corner. 'I'd get that lot to stub out the weed. I'd hate to have to arrest them all for illegal possession of cannabis.'

'Right away,' nodded Pendrie, confusion and embarrassment on his face. 'I hadn't realized they were smoking it.'

But it didn't sound convincing.

An hour later, the detectives had completed their initial inquiries at the school, several other staff having supported Pendrie's story about the headteacher's state of mind. Disturbingly for the officers, they had not experienced much in the way of loyalty towards a man who was clearly losing his grip of the situation and had started to alienate key members of staff with what they saw as his overbearing desire to exert control over every aspect of the school. Even though their testimony echoed John Pendrie's comments, none of it changed Blizzard's low opinion of the deputy headteacher, having taken an instant dislike to him, something he reiterated as he and the sergeant walked along the tree-lined drive to the front gate.

Just as Blizzard was getting into full flow, they saw a tall man marching along the main road. Aged in his mid-forties, everything about him said ex-military, his proud bearing, his ramrod-straight back, his long, purposeful strides, the chiselled weathered features, the short-cropped hair, the black boots, camouflage trousers and green T-shirt.

'Bloody hell,' murmured Colley. 'It's Rambo.'

'Marty Cundall,' murmured Blizzard. 'I wonder what he's doing here? Whatever it is, it's got to be bad news. Didn't you nick him once?'

'Yeah. For attacking a barman, just after he had been kicked out of the Army for putting a sergeant in hospital.'

They watched as Cundall marched up to confront them at the school gates, defiance flashing in his eyes.

'Marty,' said Blizzard, eyeing the military gear, 'hasn't anyone told you the war's over? Pray, what's a chap like you doing in a nice place like this?'

'Trying to stop these scum selling drugs,' snarled Cundall. 'It ain't right, Chief Inspector.'

'Indeed it's not, Marty. And may I say how your recourse to the forces of law and order does you credit even if it is somewhat unexpected. Why so interested?'

'My son is in the sixth form.'

'We've just been in the common room but we didn't see him. Was he in camouflage?'

'This ain't no laughing matter, Chief Inspector. Them toerags....'

'By which I assume you mean Eddie Barton and his cronies?'

'You know what I think about drugs, Chief Inspector, and they duffed my lad up last week when he told them to stop dealing.'

'Very community-spirited,' said Blizzard.

'That bastard Barton thumped him, Chief Inspector.'

'Perhaps he should leave it to the police next time,' replied Blizzard.

'Pha!' snorted Cundall. 'What good would that do? I told your Constable Fearnley what was happening a month ago and what did he do?'

'I really would like to know,' murmured Blizzard.

'Nothing, that's what he did. Nothing! Waste of time relying on the police! But I stopped 'em alright.'

'And how,' said Blizzard, trying not to appear too interested, 'did you do that, Marty?'

'I waited for him a few days ago – down by the church-yard.' He was selling heroin there so I belted him. He squealed like a stuck pig, I don't mind admitting,' and he grinned proudly, showing crooked, yellowed teeth.

'You might regret admitting it', said Blizzard coolly. 'You

see, last night someone attacked him again – only this time he did not get the chance to squeal. Sergeant, please be so good as to place the handcuffs upon our Mr Cundall, will you…?'

CHAPTER **SEVEN**

On the face of it, the involvement of Marty Cundall in the inquiry could not be good news for the detectives. Although Blizzard and Colley regarded him as an oddity with his fatigues and military bearing, they never made the mistake of under-estimating him. That would be dangerous because Marty Cundall was dangerous. A wily character, wary of the police and prepared to intimidate criminal associates into silence, Cundall had always had contacts within the city's under-world. His connections grew from a strong loyalty to childhood friends from his days on the city's housing estates, boys who in adulthood developed into criminal kingpins, running rackets ranging from drugs and prosti-tution to DSS fraud, rackets that spread tentacles way beyond Hafton's borders.

Although Marty was not a major figure – he did not have the brains for that – he was known to be a low-level fixer for some of the gangs, who appreciated that during his time in the Army he had been taught how to harness his violent streak. In someone dedicated to the common good, and Blizzard had received help from several former soldiers in his time, such a training and sense of responsi-bility was to be welcomed but in someone gone to the bad, like Marty, it always meant trouble. Blizzard always reminded his officers not to regard Marty too lightly, saying that if you judged someone by their friends, you had to view him with the utmost respect.

Although the involvement of such a character in their inquiries presented problems, on the other hand it presented an opportunity. Frustrated at the code of silence that protected the criminal underworld, Ronald and Blizzard had long since been debating ways of making inroads into the gangs' activities. Times had changed in the city: the crime families from the sixties and seventies had gradually lost their influence as new teams moved in and started dealing in drugs, something the older villains tended to frown on. Now with the old-timers' power on the wane in the early nineties, the new gangs were drawing up new rules, enforced by people like Marty Cundall, and the police were desperate to curtail their operations. There had been a number of top-level meetings with the Regional Crime Squad – meetings attended by Ronald and Blizzard – but as with all criminal enterprises, the roads to the big players were like impenetrable mazes. Every corner turned ended in a blank wall so the arrest of Marty Cundall, for all it complicated things, also held great promise.

Unfortunately, Marty Cundall didn't do promise. The officers' interview with him early that afternoon soon dashed any hopes they might have had of a breakthrough. Not that it was a surprise; privately, Blizzard always knew that there was no way Cundall was responsible for the killing. In his experience, murder suspects did not usually march up to him with a big sign saying 'It's a fair cop, guv, slap the cuffs on, I'll come quietly.' And Cundall's horror when he heard that Eddie Barton was dead and suddenly realized the compromising nature of his comments outside the school was too genuine to be faked.

Indeed, terrified at the predicament in which he found himself, he initially clammed up in the interview room at Abbey Road, refusing to answer questions until his lawyer arrived. When the solicitor did arrive, Cundall reluctantly once again admitted attacking Eddie Barton but vehemently denied following that up with the murderous assault in the graveyard. A quick check with members of his family was enough to confirm that, just as he had claimed, he had indeed been tucked up in bed following an evening session in the gymnasium at the time Eddie Barton was having his brains dashed out. Although Blizzard knew that Cundall's family would instinctively lie to protect him if needed, on this occasion he suspected they were telling the truth. He was not exactly surprised. Marty Cundall was many things but bright was not one of them; devising an inventive plan like dressing up as a ghost to terrify his enemies was beyond his limited imagination. Marty Cundall, as he had displayed with his earlier attack, took a more straightforward approach to these matters.

So, it was as a disappointed Blizzard and Colley were walking along the corridor from the interview room, having decided to charge Cundall with the assault on Eddie Barton then release him, that things took a somewhat surreal turn.

'Marty was never a goer,' Blizzard was saying. 'But what worries me is that he represents a bigger problem.'

'Which is?'

'He may be a headcase – correction, is a headcase – but he's genuinely angered by our failure to crack down on the drug dealing. And he's probably not the only one. We may well be looking at some kind of vigilante action here.'

'Yeah, but Marty's not exactly typical of the people of Heston, is he now?' said the sergeant.

'Maybe not but nevertheless he does represent the way they are feeling, David. And if a lot of people feel the way he does....'

He got no further because Chris Ramsey appeared at the end of the corridor.

'Sir!' he shouted. 'There's a historian wants a chat with you. He's in your office.'

'Do you know,' said Blizzard, turning to his sergeant. 'I could have sworn he said there was a historian to see us.'

'So could I,' nodded Colley as they approached the DI, who had a gleam in his eye. 'Did you order one, guv?'

'No, I'm trying to give them up,' said Blizzard as he walked towards Ramsey and eyed him suspiciously. 'A what?'

'A historian,' repeated the DI.

'That's what I thought you said. Pray, why would I want to talk to a historian, Chris?'

'This is genuine,' grinned Ramsey. 'Chap called Bob Chatterton – says he has useful information about the Vengeance Man.'

'If this is some kind of wind-up, Chris, I am not in the mood to....'

'No, it's genuine,' protested Ramsey, showing an unaccustomed sense of comedy and winking at Colley.

'Marvellous,' sighed Blizzard to the sergeant as they followed Ramsey down the corridor. 'Here I am trying to solve a murder and some loony wants to talk to me about bleeding history.'

'What with your trip to school and now this you are learning so much today,' replied Colley, an impish smile on his face as they entered the office. 'Your mother would be proud of you, guv.'

Blizzard pretended to be annoyed at the quip but Colley had known him long enough to recognize when the chief inspector was playing along with the joke. However, that did not mean that Blizzard was happy at the thought of wasting time and his mood was not improved when he walked into his room to see Bob Chatterton sitting with a large number of documents spread over the chief inspector's desk.

'What the...?' exclaimed Blizzard.

The historian stood up and extended a bony hand. Blizzard declined to take it, sat down heavily in his chair and eyed Chatterton dubiously. Aged in his early fifties, he was a tall man, thin and rangy; unkinder souls would say scrawny. The brown hair was thinning on top and he blinked at them owlishly from behind thick-rimmed glasses, his piggy little eyes bright and alert. His attire did not inspire much enthusiasm in the chief inspector, either; brown cords, a threadbare grey jumper and a brown jacket with patches over worn sleeves. Affronted by the chief inspector's refusal to shake hands, Chatterton sat back down and eyed the officers with some confusion.

'I have come to help you,' he began in his high-pitched voice. 'The least you could do is shake my....'

'Actually,' said Blizzard, eyeing with chagrin the papers spread across a desk that he had only just cleared of paperwork, 'the least I could do is kick you out for making a mess of my office. What do you want, Mr Chatterton? I am very busy.'

'I appreciate that,' nodded Chatterton furiously, his spectacles slipping down his nose, forcing him to push them back with a finger. 'But I have useful information. I have kept my counsel until now but this dreadful news about the young man in the graveyard changes everything.'

'Go on,' sighed Blizzard.

'I am the secretary of the Heston Historical Society,' began Chatterton, waiting for them to show how impressed they were.

They weren't and they didn't.

'And as such,' he continued, undeterred, 'I have become quite an expert....'

He paused and gave them another hopeful look, which was wiped off his face by Blizzard's glowering expression. Blizzard didn't like experts. Never had, never would.

'Well, anyway, yes,' stuttered Chatterton, temporarily thrown out of his stride. 'Yes, well, you see, I believe that the Vengeance Man, as the media would have it, is actually one John Ignatius White.'

All the officers looked at him with renewed interest. A name. That's what they were after, a name for the killer and with Marty Cundall out of the picture, an identity would be very welcome indeed. Particularly given that Arthur Ronald had asked Blizzard for an update three times that day already, always a sign that the chief constable was getting twitchy.

'And who, pray, is this John Ignatius White?' asked Blizzard, hoping against hope that this was a genuine breakthrough.

Some hope.

'Well,' announced Chatterton proudly, 'he lived more than 300 years ago and....'

'For God's sake!' exclaimed Blizzard, the day's frustrations combining explosively with his lack of sleep.

The chief inspector glared at the startled Chatterton then shot an accusing look at the DI.

'Why did you let this nutter in, Chris? We've got enough on our hands without....'

'Please hear him out,' said Ramsey quickly.

'Kick him out, more like,' snapped Blizzard but something in the DI's tone of voice made him pause as the chief inspector recalled his mistake in dismissing Ramsey's earlier concerns about the Vengeance Man.

'Alright,' he nodded reluctantly but jabbed a finger at Chatterton. 'Ten minutes, pal, that's all, though ... and get these bloody papers cleared away.'

Chatterton hurriedly scooped the documents into his battered briefcase and began his story. It turned out that Chatterton, a former history teacher, had founded the Heston Historical Society a decade before. During his research into something else, he came across the story of John Ignatius White, and found himself fascinated by the tale.

Despite his irritation, Blizzard, who had a somewhat unusual pastime himself in that he lovingly restored steam locomotives, could appreciate Chatterton's enthusiasm for the subject and, for all his scepticism, found himself gradually increasingly engrossed by the story. At one point, Chatterton stopped and reminded him that the ten minutes were up but the chief inspector amazed Colley and delighted Ramsey by waving away the comment and urging him to go on.

John White, explained Chatterton, was a corn merchant, living in Heston, then a tiny village, in 1652, a couple of years after Cromwell created his Protectorate following his victory over the Royalists in the English Civil War. Cromwell's triumph heralded in a golden age of Puritanism, in stark contrast to the decadent years of monarchy that had gone before, and John White was as Puritan as they came. A tall, imposing man with fierce religious beliefs and well-defined views on the way people should live, his devotion to personal purity manifested itself in a god-fearing life and adherence to a strict code of conduct, which he expected those around him to observe rigorously.

However, his beliefs were increasingly challenged by the actions of a local band of young footpads who eked out a living through highway robbery in the highways and byways surrounding Heston. Everyone knew who they were but seemed reluctant to tackle them, frightened of their reputation for violence. Not so John White, who was one of their victims, beaten over the head with a cudgel and robbed of his money just outside the village, followed a few days later by his nineteen-year-old son, whom they battered to within an inch of his life for what little money he had with him. The incident was the final straw for John White, who had already been plotting his revenge.

A few days later, Heston witnessed the appearance of a truly terrifying figure, dressed in black boots, a long black coat and with a wide-brimmed black hat, striding along the streets and roaring dire threats against those who broke the Lord's law. But this was no spectre, this was John Ignatius White in full flow, invoking the power of the Lord above in his crusade against the wrongdoers. His idea of Christian love and forgiveness seemed somewhat twisted, however, and over the next few weeks, three of the footpads met grisly deaths, one nailed by his hands to a tree in a nearby wood, the second discovered lying at the bottom of a farm track with a battered skull and the third bludgeoned to death with some form of club as he walked home through the countryside late one night. That left just one of the gang and several weeks later, having gone into hiding, he emerged somewhat timorously to meet his death in Heston graveyard, his skull shattered into fragments with a piece of stone, snapped off one of the gravestones with terrific force.

By now all three detectives were listening intently, struck by the similarities with the Vengeance Man and the death of Eddie Barton, and Blizzard had picked up the phone and ordered that all his calls be diverted. After the death of the final gang member, Chatterton told them, assuring the officers that the story was all chronicled in the documents he had brought in, a number of soldiers arrived from Hafton to arrest John White so that he could stand trial. There was a brawl in the market-place as a group of local people tried to prevent him being taken away; they had come to regard him as a hero, righting wrongs and punishing those whom the Lord would have punished. They clashed violently with the soldiers, during which one of the villagers received injuries from which he later died. Two soldiers were also badly hurt.

During the chase that ensued, White managed to escape his pursuers and make his way down to Heston's small river harbour where, badly wounded in the shoulder by one of the riflemen, he staggered along the outer wall for a moment or two before toppling into the river, never to be seen again. His body was never recovered and all those who saw his death swore that there had been no splash.

For a century afterwards there had been stories that John White was still seen at dead of night, returning to the scene of his crimes, striding through Heston and uttering his baleful threats against those who outraged the forces of god-fearing decency. Over time, the stories had gradually faded away but Bob Chatterton had discovered them during his research and delved deeper for a book that he was now hoping to write on the subject.

'And just to add to the coincidence,' he concluded, revelling in the impact that his story had had, 'I think if you go back to Heston churchyard you will discover that the area around the gravestone on which young Eddie Barton perished includes the last resting place of none other than John Ingatius White.'

'But I thought you said his body was never found,' said Colley quickly.

'Indeed, sergeant,' nodded Chatterton, glancing at Colley, who was leaning against the closed door. 'Very astute of you but the villagers, assuming him to be dead and deeply appreciative of what he had done for them, gave him the decency of a Christian burial anyway. It is said that the coffin contains some of his clothes and other personal belongings but since no one has ever exhumed it I cannot say if that is so.'

'Well,' said Blizzard, tipping back in his chair and eyeing the historian intently. 'It's quite a story, Mr Chatterton, but I do hope you are not suggesting that Eddie Barton had his head stoved in by a 300-year-old ghost?'

'I am not that deluded,' smiled Chatterton. 'But perhaps the ghost of John White did have a part to play.'

'Oh, come on!' exclaimed Colley.

'From what I hear on the radio your Mister Barton had a serious head injury. Perhaps he was not attacked – what if he fell after seeing the ghost?'

'Indeed,' murmured Blizzard.

He had entertained some doubts himself when the post-mortem failed to rule out for definite the theory that Barton had stumbled and accidentally hit his head on the stone. Blizzard had asked about that at the examination and the pathologist said it was unlikely given the force of the blow but that it was not totally out of the question. Admittedly, it remained the least likely of the theories but it had yet to be discounted and Blizzard knew that truth was often stranger than fiction. His mind went back to the death of an elderly spinster, a retired geography teacher, early in his

CID career. She had been found lying in her living room, soaked in blood and with a nasty head injury. Adding to the suspicious nature of her death, one of the rear windows in her cottage was broken and there were signs that the house had been searched by an intruder.

CID treated it as a murder for several days until it emerged that she had fallen accidentally, striking her head on a table edge, causing a massive hemorrhage. The broken window, it turned out, was caused by a burglar who broke in, discovered to his horror the body on the living room floor, and after a cursory search of the living room fled the scene, keeping his secret until police tracked him down. The incident taught Blizzard never to assume anything, a rule he was acutely aware that he had broken in dismissing the Vengeance Man when Chris Ramsey brought the story to his attention.

The chief inspector was also intrigued by the amount of reasoning the bookish historian seemed to have put into his consideration of the death of Eddie Barton. In his experience, people like that usually knew much more than they were letting on and the annals of criminal history, which he studied enthusiastically, were crammed with tales of killers who deliberately drew attention to themselves as part of the game.

'So,' said Blizzard, changing the subject, keen to disguise his interest in Chatterton himself until he could discuss it with his colleagues, 'who else knows about this story? Who else have you told?'

'Not many people,' said Chatterton, shaking his head vigorously. 'I only came across it by accident and, because I am keen to write this book, I have kept it fairly quiet. I don't want anyone else beating me to the punch.'

'A poor choice of words,' said Blizzard. 'But have you told anyone at all about our Mister White?'

'Oh, yes, I gave a talk to the historical society a few weeks ago,' nodded Chatterton, adding confidently. 'They are friends. I know that none of them would steal my idea.'

'OK,' said Blizzard, standing up and extending a hand, a gesture not lost on the beaming historian. 'Thank you very much for coming in, Mr Chatterton. It has been most enlightening.'

'Thank you, Chief Inspector,' said Chatterton, gathering up his papers and clearly delighted with the change of Blizzard's demeanour. 'I appreciate being given more than ten minutes of your precious time.'

'See him out will you, please, David,' said Blizzard.

'Well?' asked Ramsey eagerly, after they had gone. 'What do you think?'

'I think,' and Blizzard's eyes narrowed, 'that I want to find out everything we can about our Mister Chatterton's own history....'

CHAPTER **EIGHT**

John Blizzard's growing interest in Bob Chatterton was based not just on a detective's instinct that something was not quite right but also on his admiration for the passion the historian displayed for his subject. It was almost, Blizzard felt, as if he were suspecting one of his own and, for all his professionalism, he felt a touch uneasy at the thought.

The reason the chief inspector felt that way was because Chatterton's enthusiasm for Cromwellian history mirrored his own for the Golden Age of Steam and, in particular, a locomotive he called The Old Lady. Blizzard's fascination for the subject stretched back to a grandfather who was a shedmaster in industrial Yorkshire in the pre-war years and a father who worked for a while as a train driver. Also, when the family lived in rural Lincolnshire before his father's job took them, reluctantly, north to grimy urban Hafton, the young Blizzard used to love standing at the bottom of the garden of their cottage to watch the steam engines thunder past. Sometimes, if he was lucky, the drivers caught sight of him perched on the fence, waved and gave long pulls on the whistle.

It was a sound that always raised goosebumps for Blizzard and an interest that had been sustained into adult life, which was why, as evening fell that day, the chief inspector could be found unlocking the padlock to a corrugated iron engine shed on wasteland beyond the railway lines at the edge of the city centre. Entering the shed was like entering another world. Behind was the hum and throb of the city – which Blizzard often felt like fleeing in search of somewhere more peaceful, a throwback, he assumed, to his rural upbringing. Before him, dimly illuminated by a stark single light bulb, was a tangle of scrap metal and old rusted tools, in the middle of which stood Blizzard's great love.

Fifteen years ago, he had helped form the Hafton Railway Appreciation Society, a small group of enthusiastic volunteers who used their spare time to restore steam loco-motives. Blizzard was noted for his remarkable grasp of the subject, a legacy, he always used to say, of a childhood spent devouring books about steam, and even the group of old railmen in the society tended to bow to his superior knowledge. Of all the plaudits Blizzard had received in his life – from fellow officers, judges, grateful victims' families and even the odd grudging villain – it was the approbation of the railmen that he most valued.

The engine before him in the shed was very important to Blizzard, who, now rubbing his hands together in the cold, was busy switching on the small heater, filling the kettle and clambering into grease-stained blue overalls. The Silver Flyer had plied the line between the city and the Midlands for many years until taken out of commission in the 1960s as the great age of steam died. For a long time, no one seemed to know where she was, even though she had lain, sad and neglected in the shed behind the main station all that time.

Blizzard had stumbled across the dilapidated building while investigating a serious assault on a man crossing the wasteland. He had stood in amazement as he scraped off the rust to reveal the locomotive's nameplate. It did not take him long to persuade society members to raise the cash to buy her from her owner, who was relieved to get her off his hands. They set out to renovate her, driven by the dream that one day The Flyer would steam again. That day was a long way away yet but that realization did not diminish the ardour of the enthusiasts who gave up their free time to lavish love and attention on her.

Blizzard did not broadcast his pastime but it was well enough known in police and criminal circles in the city. However, those who took the mickey out of the hobby – usually not within his earshot – should have realized that the engine was a important crime-fighting tool as well because it was here, in the chilly rundown shed and surrounded by relics of Hafton's industrial past, that the chief inspector sifted through the facts of his cases and came up with his conclusions. Many a crime had been solved during his sessions with the Old Lady. And it was the need to think away from ringing telephones and the constant demands on his time that had driven him from the police station and down to the shed shortly after six that Thursday night.

As he worked to free a couple of obdurate screws, cursing as he banged his fingers more than once, Blizzard reflected on what he had learned over the past few hours. It had been a dispiriting day. Given that the link between the disappearance of the headteacher and the events surrounding the Vengeance Man was Eddie Barton, it had seemed sensible to concentrate on him and his fellow gang members right from the start. Very quickly, Blizzard had detailed two of his detectives to find out everything they knew about the dead teenager. Despite experiencing a disconcerting wall of silence about his more recent activities, many of those to whom they spoke clearly frightened of Barton and his associates, the detectives had nevertheless been able to build up a reasonable picture of the kind of person he was.

Their initial reports made for salutary reading when they arrived on Blizzard's desk and he could not help feeling that, crime or no crime, the murder of Eddie Barton had done society a favour. Not that society had done him many favours. Eddie Barton was a thoroughly nasty piece of work – but it had not always been that way. He had been born into a loving, stable, working-class family but his father, a toolmaker, died of cancer when the boy was nine, the first of two significant events that dramatically changed the course of his life. The loss of his father had a seismic effect on the youngster and he rapidly went off the rails, becoming withdrawn at home and disruptive at primary school, where he was warned several times by his exasperated teachers for bullying children smaller than himself.

However, after a couple of years his disruptive behaviour started to calm down and there were real hopes that he could make something of his life after all. Which was when his mother remarried, the second event that shifted the course of his life. It was not a happy choice for either mother or child. The stepfather, all smiles and gifts when wooing her, and lavishing attention on the youngster to win his trust, turned out to be a monster who treated his wife like a slave and mother and son as punchbags during his frequent drunken rages. That Eddie's mother left him after four years of abuse seemed to make little difference to the boy. Neither did the move from their terraced house on the north side of the city, where the teenager had spent all his life, to a house on one of the new estates in Heston.

His mother had seen it as representing a fresh start and had saved every penny to be able to afford the mortgage, taking two jobs to ensure she could meet the payments. The house may have been a small box but to Mrs Barton it was a palace. Not so for her son; Eddie, now an unruly and muscular teenager, hated the middle-class life and felt increasingly out of place. His sense of alienation was not helped by constant clashes with the neighbours. Old before their time, they frowned on Eddie and constantly rebuked him for playing football in the street in the evening and allegedly damaging plants and cars with the ball, something Eddie always denied when questioned by his unhappy mother.

As he read the reports, Blizzard was struck yet again how society could create the very monsters of which it was

so frightened. Deeply unhappy and with a growing resent-
ment of everyone and everything, Eddie Barton ran out of
control and looked around for role models other than his
mother, who was increasingly depressed and unable to
exert control over her wayward son. Unfortunately, those
role models were Roger Colclough, Paul Moody and
Raymond Ransome, whom he met in his first year at
Heston Comprehensive.

Detectives investigating their backgrounds had uncov-
ered similar stories of broken homes, fathers who had
walked out, a lack of parental control and a total rejection
of the social mores of middle-class life on Heston's new
housing estates. All of them big lads, and rejecting everything about their backgrounds, they made their own rules,
their fists and feet given free reign as bullies at Heston
Comprehensive School. As they reached their final year at
the school, they moved into drug dealing, initially selling
cannabis to fellow pupils. The way they defended their
territory with violence meant they were regarded by pupils
and teachers alike as the school's most feared bullies.

Barton's grief-stricken mother, racked by guilt that she
had not done more to help her son, told Detective Sergeant
David Tulley that she had frequently despaired for his
future but that she felt powerless to change things. Eddie,
she said, did not listen to her protestations and clearly had
no respect for her and when he fell in with Colclough,
Moody and Ransome, it was her worst fears come true. It
was a story that the officers found repeated by the other
boys' parents as they sat, hand-wringing and bewildered,
in their trim and tidy, dust-free living rooms with nice
ornaments and pretty prints on the walls. The events
surrounding Eddie Barton and his associates were the ulti-
mate middle-class nightmare. That it had all been kept
quiet, a drama enacted behind attractive front doors and
short-cropped handkerchief-sized front lawns, was another
striking feature. Blizzard never ceased to be amazed by the
secret torments concealed behind people's desperate

attempts to present a respectable façade to their neighbours when their lives were crumbling about them.

Having left school and continued their involvement with the drugs trade, Barton and his friends soon progressed to selling heroin. Barton and Colclough moved into a flat together and the other two also left home, renting bedsits and maintaining the slightest of links with their families, usually only when they needed some money. At the time of Barton's death, he had not spoken to his mother for a year. For the other parents, contact had only been sporadic.

Mrs Barton, a meek woman still bearing a scar on her cheek from her second husband's final vicious assault, was finding the revelations following her son's death hard to handle. She knew he was into bad ways but the extent of what she was hearing had horrified her. What she did tell Tulley, between sobs, was that shortly after her son left school, she had heard that Eddie, probably with the other boys, had tracked down his former stepfather to a flat on the other side of the city and had beaten him up with base-ball bats in revenge for the way he had behaved towards Barton and his mother. On returning to Abbey Road, Tulley checked the records and discovered that one of the local bobbies remembered the incident but said no prosecution was brought because the stepfather declined to press charges even though he spent two days in hospital. The constable said he suspected the stepfather was terrified of a repeat visit but without his testimony, the PC was forced, reluctantly, to drop the case.

It was a recurring trend that alarmed Blizzard as he read on, sitting in his office early that afternoon, his mood not helped by the gloomy skies outside and the occasional bursts of squally rain sweeping up the river from the North Sea. What was increasingly clear to the chief inspector was that everyone was running scared of the gang, which is why despite extensive inquiries, police were no nearer to discovering their hiding place. There was no sign of them at their last known addresses and checks at their usual haunts had failed to turn up any pointers to their location.

Time and time again, associates feigned ignorance but their eyes revealed that fear was the main motivator for their blank faces and non-committal answer to queries from frustrated detectives. Blizzard found this all deeply disconcerting; he had come across people who exerted this kind of hold on people before but they had been hardened, experienced gangsters rather than a bunch of teenagers not long out of nappies. That they had built such an empire under police noses in such a short time without much having been done to stop them concerned the chief inspector.

All these thoughts added to the pressure on Blizzard, who having read his detectives' report with regular disbelieving shakes of the head and a growing sense of unease, picked up the phone shortly after three. Having set his detectives off on their new tasks, Blizzard set out to discover what had gone wrong with the policing in Heston to let things reach a sorry state. It was clear to him that there had been a terrible failing of everyone involved. People, police officers among them, were clearly aware of what the gang were doing but nobody had done anything about it.

No wonder, thought Blizzard grimly, that Marty Cundall and the Vengeance Man – whoever he may be – had taken the law into their own hands. He could not really blame them, he thought grimly as he had driven to Heston police station to talk to the community constable, Fearnley. And if he had sympathy with Cundall's standpoint, goodness knows what ferment was bubbling under in the community at large, thought Blizzard.

His examination of PC Fearnley had done nothing to improve his mood and Blizzard's face clouded over as he paused from his labours on the locomotive and recalled the unsatisfactory meeting that afternoon. As Colley had said, Fearnley came over as a somewhat feckless young man but, more than that, he also appeared unsure as to what to do with the intelligence he was picking up in his role as one of the community bobbies in Heston. An inexperienced officer, Fearnley told Blizzard that he had known about the drug dealing and the other activities in which Barton and his gang had been involved, including burglaries, car theft and assaults, but that nobody in the community seemed prepared to stand up as witnesses against them so he felt powerless to do anything about it.

Fearnley did not say as much, but clearly hinted, that he had also felt somewhat isolated in Heston, working out of the small village police station that had had its uniformed beat officers reduced from five to just himself in the last round of cutbacks by a chief constable under pressure from the police authority. He also intimated – as far as he dared, given that his inspector was also sitting in the meeting – at a lack of support from his senior officers. According to Fearnley, he had passed what he knew up the chain of command but was told that without evidence arrests were out of the question.

While angry that such a situation meant the police were viewed as impotent by large sections of the local community, the chief inspector had nevertheless been forced to admit that there was something in what Fearnley said. Blizzard – who had interviewed the constable at Heston police station in the company of uniformed Inspector Edwards – had concluded by rebuking the young man for not communicating his difficulties more forcefully but also acknowledged that the blame should not all be heaped on his shoulders, something he repeated in typically blunt terms to an increasingly irate Inspector Edwards in a private meeting before he left Heston to return to Abbey Road. Edwards, for his part, was angered by the criticism and the fact that a CID officer should rebuke an uniformed officer and the upshot was that Blizzard came away from the episode more concerned than ever. And he knew that trouble would soon be on its way after the row.

It did not take long to arrive. Blizzard paused in his labours on the engine again and scowled as he recalled the events before he left Abbey Road for the shed. Blizzard had expressed his concerns in a conversation behind closed doors in Arthur Ronald's office shortly before five that afternoon. The detective chief superintendent had been watching the unfolding events of the afternoon with concerns of his own and had asked to see the chief inspector before things escalated.

'You're making waves,' Ronald said calmly, handing Blizzard a mug of tea.

'Don't pull the top brass thing on me,' protested Blizzard. 'This is a police cock-up.'

'A point I understand you made to Charlie Edwards in somewhat forceful terms.'

The comment was accompanied by a gentle smile from the superintendent.

'I hope you were in the right.'

'Too bloody right I was!' exclaimed Blizzard. 'The slippery old bugger was trying to shift the blame – too near retirement that one. Should get rid of him – get Matty Rylance in to do the job.'

'Well, for your information, the moment you left Heston, Charlie Edwards complained to his super about your attitude,' said Ronald, having only moments earlier come off the phone from his angry counterpart in uniform. 'And our Mr Bond is not very happy with you.'

'Billy bloody Bond,' snorted Blizzard at the mention of the man who had overall command for uniform in the southern county divisions, Western among them.

Leaning forward earnestly, he said, 'Listen, Arthur, the more I learn about this the more I am worried about the way we have handled it. These lads have been a law unto themselves and we have not done enough to stop them, if you ask me.'

'I know,' nodded Ronald, who despite his need to maintain diplomatic relations between CID and uniform, had been equally aghast at some of the comments he was hearing from Chief Supt Bond, who appeared to be more focused on defending himself than addressing the issues. 'Young Fearnley should have....'

'Don't just blame him. That's too easy. There's a chain of command here, Arthur. He's a young lad and he should not have been left out there on his own. No one seems to have been helping him, Arthur. Billy Bond may not like it but if uniform had got their act together we could have stood on this when these lads first got into heroin dealing.'

'And CID?' asked Ronald, eyeing him shrewdly. 'What about our act?'

'All of us,' nodded Blizzard firmly, taking a sip of tea. 'But to be fair we do have a defence. A couple of our lads had picked up bits of info and told the Drugs Squad instead of passing it up the line here. We should have investigated it ourself. I will be talking to Chris Ramsey about that. He's supposed to be on top of these things.'

'Don't stir things up too much,' warned Ronald. 'We've got enough on our plate as it is - the last thing we want is hacked-off officers.'

'I take the point,' nodded Blizzard, 'but what's worse than hacked-off officers is hacked-off members of the public. If we do not do something and do it fast we are in danger of losing control of this situation.'

'We can agree on that,' nodded Ronald, pursing his lips.

Like Blizzard, since the murder he had received several phone calls from anxious residents of Heston, a couple of lawyers among them, bending his ear about police inaction.

'We've already got people in Heston jumping up and down because we did not arrest Barton and his cronies,' continued Blizzard earnestly, 'plus we have the Vengeance Man taking the law into his own hands and now I hear there's a public meeting at the school on Friday night to kick off about it.'

'To which you and I are going,' said Ronald.

'Yeah, like....' replied Blizzard dismissively.

'To which you and I are going,' repeated Ronald firmly.

Blizzard thought about protesting then nodded his assent. Friends or not, he recognized an order from Ronald when he heard it.

'If you say so.'

'And I don't expect you to stand up and tell them we have failed,' added Ronald. 'Things are bad enough without you falling on your sword.'

'Don't worry, I'll behave. Besides, it's Billy Bond's sword. And if he fell on it, there is no guarantee it would get through the rolls of fat.'

'Now, now,' said Ronald, who was acutely conscious about his own constant battle with his weight.

'And he would never admit we have failed anyway, Arthur. Too busy covering his back.'

'Maybe,' grunted Ronald, acutely conscious of how exposed his own back had become.

But the chance to put one over on Bond was a sore temptation. He had little time for the portly superintendent, trying to reassure himself – as he did so often – that it was nothing to do with the fact that the men might be rivals for the next big promotion in the county. Assistant Chief Constable Ronald had a certain ring to it, he had always thought. Trouble was, Billy Bond spouted the jargon, which stuck in Arthur Ronald's throat.

'We have to win the people of Heston back,' urged Blizzard, returning Ronald's mind to the matter at hand.

'So what do you suggest?'

'Well,' and Blizzard adopted a more conciliatory tone, 'you're right, we all have to work together whatever I may think of Bond and his band of merry men and women. We need to find Barton's cronies. And before you say it, yes I know that's my job. They're lying low but now they know Barton is dead they will have to break cover. They'll either be shit scared or mad as hell, probably both.'

'Should give us the chance to nab them.'

'In theory. Also, I think uniform should mount high

profile patrols in the area, particularly near the school, placate some angry parents, that sort of thing. A patrol car sitting outside the school as people turn up for the meeting might not be a bad thing.'

'Sounds sensible.'

'I would suggest this to Billy Bond myself but....' and Blizzard gave his superintendent a cheesy grin.

'Yeah, I'll do it,' said Ronald hurriedly.

'Oh, there's another thing. Colley got a call from one of his informants this afternoon. First one brave enough to speak to us. Guy was terrified but he reckons Barton and his gang are the same ones doing over the shops.'

'Is he sure?' asked Ronald with interest.

'Makes sense, doesn't it? I was beginning to wonder the same thing myself. The violence shown by the robbers links in with what we have heard about Barton and his gang. If the informant is right, that throws a whole new complexion on the case, doesn't it now?'

'It does indeed,' agreed Ronald, picking up the phone and winking at the chief inspector. 'Glenys, can you get me Billy bloody Bond please ... yes, you, heard me right....'

Blizzard was still chuckling at the joke a couple of hours later as he pottered around the engine shed and tried to make sense of it all. And as he worked, and intrigued as he was by Bob Chatterton's carefully thought-out interest in the murder and Marty Cundall's readiness to use violence, Blizzard nevertheless came round to thinking about the main person on his list of suspects, the missing head-teacher, the nervy Mervyn Howard. Surely, he mused, as he clattered about in the corner of the shed, cursing that he had not bothered to replace the wrench in its usual place last time he used it, a headteacher would not resort to killing ex-pupils because they were selling drugs at the school gate?

Ah, but what if the headteacher believed the police were not doing anything to protect him and his school, what if he was suffering some sort of breakdown, as Pendrie had hinted, and what, this last thought prompted by the lack of concern shown by the teachers, if Mervyn Howatch felt he had lost not just the support of his pupils but also his staff? And what if he was convinced that he had also lost the support of a local education authority that seemed determined to close Heston Comp? Add to that his fears for his health and it could be argued that he was no longer someone thinking rationally.

Blizzard recalled telling Colley once that people need something to anchor them. Take away their anchor, as had happened with Mervyn Howatch, and they were drifting out of control in the sea, at the mercy of the currents and the tides. And if that was the case, he had said, anything was possible. Such a maritime analogy had seemed appropriate, given the seafaring past of Heston. Blizzard's dark thoughts were disturbed by the grating of the door to the shed and Colley popped his head round.

'Are you and your lady decent?' he quipped. 'I'd hate to disturb you polishing some fropple sprockets or whatever you call them.'

'Come in,' smiled Blizzard, nodding at the sports bag slung over the sergeant's shoulder. 'I take it you've been to rugby practice?'

'Yeah, big inter-force game on Sunday. We're up against Lincolnshire.'

'The yellowbellies, eh?'

'I'm not sure I'd call them that to their face,' said Colley doubtfully, 'last time we played them they....'

'It's what Lincolnshire people are called,' sighed Blizzard.

'Does that make you a yellowbelly then?'

'Yes, but I don't expect to hear any jokes on the subject,' said Blizzard. 'What brings you here anyway?'

'Superintendent Bond asked me to say how much he admires and respects you and wonders if you would like to join him and Mrs Bond for dinner one night,' grinned Colley impishly.

'You heard then?'

'The whole bloody station has heard,' said Colley delightedly. 'In fact, I got a call from a couple of lads over at East asking if it was true. Most of them think Bond is a dick-head anyway. Same for Edwards. And that's uniform as well as CID.'

'Thank goodness I don't hear what they say about me behind my back,' muttered Blizzard, secretly delighted at the news that the troops supported his stand. 'Anyway, what does bring you here?'

'A bit of a development,' said Colley. 'Tulley called as I was heading for the pub after practice … perfect timing as usual. They've found the headteacher's car down by the river.'

'No rest for the wicked,' sighed Blizzard, wiping his hand with an oily rag and beginning to struggle out of his overalls. 'Let's go and look see.'

Twenty minutes later they were standing on the river-bank a quarter of a mile downstream from Heston harbour. While Colley and the forensics team examined the vehicle by torchlight in the wooded car park where it had been abandoned, Blizzard wandered off a few yards through the trees and stood on the shingle shoreline, gazing out over the river at the chemical complex on the south side, the twinkling lights reflected in the dark waters of the Haft. Apart from the engine shed, it was his favourite spot for contemplation. Listening to the lapping of the river and the distant hum of traffic and occasional fog horn from the city, he murmured, 'Where are you, Mr Howatch?'

He turned at the crunch of shoes on pebbles as his sergeant approached.

'Well?' he asked.

'Not much really,' replied Colley, turning his collar up as a chill breeze blew in off the water. 'No sign of anything untoward. No keys in the lock. No final message. No empty bottle of pills. Nothing.'

'Is the engine warm?'

'Na. He's long gone,' and the sergeant nodded at the river. 'Into there, perhaps?'

'Maybe.'

'You still reckon he's the Vengeance Man?' asked Colley.

'He's the best suspect we have,' nodded Blizzard, staring moodily out over the river again. 'And if he did do the murder and he didn't chuck himself in the river, I would not like to be Eddie Barton's little mates tonight, would you...?'

CHAPTER **NINE**

I t was a more circumspect John Pendrie who met
Blizzard and Colley in the headteacher's office at
Heston Comprehensive School on the Friday morning.
Seated in Mervyn Howatch's chair and dressed noticeably
smarter in a dark suit, he gave the impression of a man
who was exactly where he wanted to be. From the relatively sheltered position of deputy headteacher with
responsibility primarily for the sixth form, John Pendrie
had found himself catapulted into the frontline and was
enjoying the experience. Behind the laid-back exterior
lurked an ambitious man and, suddenly, it seemed that
everyone wanted a piece of him; the frustrations of years
as Mervyn Howatch's deputy melted away. John Pendrie
had become important. Life, he reflected, might be so
much easier in the backwaters but it was nowhere near as
satisfying.

'Paperwork,' he said ruefully, gesturing to the pile of
reports stacked up on the desk. 'The bane of a headteacher's life.'

'Acting headteacher surely,' said Blizzard quickly, split
between thinking of how his own pile of documents was
starting to grow again and struck by the easy way Pendrie
seemed to have settled into his new responsibilities.

'My apologies, acting headteacher,' said Pendrie, his
temporary elevation having made him suddenly acutely
aware of the need to make friends in high places. 'You may
have got the wrong impression of me the last time we met,

Chief Inspector. I must have sounded very unsympathetic in my comments about poor Mervyn.'

'Just a bit,' murmured Blizzard.

'I do not think I had fully realized the import of what was happening. You see, I thought Mervyn would come back fairly quickly. Now it seems he may not.'

'He may yet,' said Colley. 'We only found his car. There was no sign of him.'

'So there is still hope?'

The words were the right ones but the tone struck the wrong chord with the detectives, who could not help but feel they were witnessing an act by a disappointed man.

'Possibly,' said Blizzard guardedly. 'Actually, we wanted to talk to you about his relationship with Eddie Barton. It sounds like Mervyn had good reason to dislike him.'

'Yes, but I do hope you are not suggesting that Mervyn killed that appalling young man,' protested Pendrie.

Again right words but not convincing.

'I am not suggesting anything, Mr Pendrie,' said Blizzard, Ronald's warning about diplomacy ringing in his ears, 'but as it stands, your headteacher did have an excellent motive to go after Barton and we don't know where he was when the boy was murdered.'

'I suppose so.'

'Can you think of anything you did not tell us about Mr Howatch last time?' asked Colley.

'I don't think so,' said Pendrie blandly.

'Try harder.'

'No, nothing,' said Pendrie but he seemed unsettled by Colley's persistence.

'We know anyway,' said the sergeant.

'About what?'

'The incident involving Eddie Barton and his cronies at Mervyn's home a few weeks ago.'

'How the devil do you know about that?' Pendrie seemed surprised. 'Mervyn told your officers at the time that he did not want any more action taking.'

'Indeed he did,' said Blizzard, 'but a conscientious young bobby was so disturbed about what happened he submitted a report anyway. The sergeant here dug it out of the file. The question is why you declined to mention it.'

'She asked me not to,' said Pendrie flatly. 'Said she was not going to say anything about it.'

'She?' asked Colley.

'His wife. Said she did not want anyone to know about it. Rang me to reiterate the point.'

'Well, she changed her mind and called us first thing this morning,' said the sergeant. 'Why do you think she wanted it kept quiet?'

'It hardly looks good, does it, what with Eddie Barton dead and her husband missing? She hoped you would not find out about it.'

'It's a miracle we did,' muttered Blizzard, who had been arguing for years that the force desperately needed to upgrade its record-keeping, only to be told a new computer system would cost too much money. He determined to use this case to support his argument. They would not always get lucky.

'It doesn't look good,' agreed Colley. 'I take it Mervyn told you himself about what happened?'

'Yes. He was very shaken by it all. You see, when Barton and Colclough and the others left three years ago, Mervyn was very relieved. He seemed to grow an inch or two. They were all big lads and I did hear that Colclough once hit him when he was being expelled. Anyway, when they left, Mervyn said he never wanted to see them again. Very unusual that – he usually took a keen interest in ex-pupils.'

'But he saw Barton?'

'A few times.'

'But the most recent one, tell us about that,' said Blizzard.

'Three or four weeks ago he came in looking pretty shaky. Said he had seen Barton in the street and had a go at him for selling drugs on the wasteland behind the rec – we had picked up rumours about it from some of the pupils.'

'And what happened?'

'Barton and the others turned up outside his house a couple of nights later. Threw a brick through his window and hurled paint over his car. Mervyn has an old Morgan. He was devastated when they attacked it. We often used to joke that he loved the car more than his wife.'

'So he confronted them?'

'Yes,' nodded Pendrie. 'Silly really. He came storming out of his house and there was an altercation. Barton said he'd regret it. To the best of my knowledge, they never came back to his house but surprise, surprise, they started selling drugs outside the school.'

'And Mervyn's reaction was?'

'Horror and guilt. Thought it was his fault they targeted the school.'

'Why not let us deal with it?' asked Colley. 'We could have done something about it.'

'Mervyn was pretty disillusioned, said your lot had not dealt with things like you should have. I mean, you have not exactly done much so far have you?'

Blizzard bit his lip but said nothing. If he had spoken, it would only be to agree and he did not want those words relayed to the public meeting that evening. Things were fraught enough without that.

'Besides,' continued Pendrie, 'he did not want to make things any worse. I think he rather hoped it would all blow over.'

'Isn't that a somewhat complacent attitude?' asked the sergeant.

'Maybe. But I think he was really frightened of them. And ashamed.'

'Ashamed?'

'Yes, of being terrorized by his ex-pupils. Not a good advert for his tenure as headteacher, is it? Like I said, proud man our Mervyn.'

'And you – were you frightened of them when they were pupils here?' asked Blizzard.

Pendrie paused. For a moment the only sound in the office was the driving rain falling from the leaden skies outside as he pondered the question.

'I am not sure I like the intimation behind the question,' he said at length.

'There is no intimation,' replied the chief inspector. 'I just want an answer. Were you frightened of them?'

'No,' and Pendrie shook his head. 'You see, my approach was … how can I put it? Different. I talked to them like adults. Mervyn treated them like spoiled little children.'

'But you knew what kind of people they were, surely?' protested the sergeant.

'Everybody did but Mervyn was always insistent that he would deal with disciplinary matters. I suggested a different approach – more softly softly – but he turned me down. I was less….' and Pendrie chose his next words carefully, 'autocratic. More prepared to engage with them.'

'Self-expression again,' snorted Blizzard.

'You have to treat them like adults,' protested Pendrie. 'Even the toughest of them responds to that.'

'Well, we can see how they responded, can't we,' scowled Blizzard, 'and now young Eddie Barton is dead. Personally, I am with your headteacher on this one.'

'It's not just our responsibility,' began Pendrie. 'The parents….'

'Buck-passing,' said Blizzard dismissively, standing up and heading for the door. 'Buck-passing, Mr Pendrie….'

And he stalked from the room, leaving the sentence half-finished and hanging in the air. Colley gave Pendrie an apologetic look and followed his chief inspector out into the corridor.

'Don't you think you were a bit hard on him, guv?' asked Colley as they walked down the drive towards the car.

'Maybe,' scowled Blizzard, stopping and turning to look

at his sergeant with a troubled expression on his face. 'But something has gone terribly wrong at this school, David. And we are being left to pick up the pieces....'

CHAPTER TEN

I t was not Blizzard's fascination with John Pendrie that took him back to the school that afternoon, rather his growing interest in Bob Chatterton. Checks into the historian's background having failed to throw up anything sinister, the chief inspector nevertheless felt that it was worth time spent delving deeper into Chatterton's obsession with John Ignatius White and the way in which history seemed to be repeating itself in deadly fashion. So it was that he found himself entering the community centre, a single-storey flat-roofed red brick building next to the school. Part of the same site and used as overflow classrooms by the school, it also acted as a meeting room for local associations, one of which was the Heston Historical Society, whose members gathered every Friday afternoon at two o'clock for a cup of tea and a wander down memory lane.

Walking into the room, Blizzard saw exactly what he expected to see and something he didn't. Seated round the table were a dozen men and women, most of them aged in their sixties and seventies. The only ones who were not pensioners were Chatterton, who was sitting at the head of the room introducing the meeting, and the man next to him, a chap in his mid-forties, dressed in a sharp black suit with an immaculate red silk tie. Blizzard viewed him with interest. The rest of the assembled gathering was as he had predicted, all white hair, spectacles, faded tweed jackets and a faint aroma of cocoa and biscuits but this man was different.

He was clearly some kind of businessman, surmised Blizzard. The sharp clothes suggested that. His face – lean and clean-shaven – had the tell-tale features of the entrepreneur with alert eyes and pursed lips, which suggested impatience at wasted time, and hair, brown with flecks of grey, stylishly cut and perfectly groomed. There was definitely a sense of purpose about him, thought Blizzard. And something familiar. Blizzard had the distinct impression he knew him from somewhere but could not recall where.

'I do apologize for the intrusion, Bob', said Blizzard, nodding at Chatterton.

Politeness always went down well with these kind of people.

'That's alright, Chief Inspector,' said Chatterton, flattered by the intimate use of his first name.

'I wonder if you would mind me asking one or two questions before you start?'

'That's fine,' nodded Chatterton, his smile suggesting delight that such a man as John Blizzard should be so courteous to him, and in front of his peers as well. 'Our speaker cried off with flu. Not necessarily a bad thing....'

And he allowed himself a half smile.

'... I am not entirely sure that booking her for two hours on the medieval pottery of Lower Bustford was a good idea in hindsight.'

There were knowing chuckles from the others.

'So,' asked Chatterton, 'what would you like to know?'

Blizzard was not quite sure – his visit was really to have a second look at Bob Chatterton as he tried to work him out. The experience so far had tended to confirm his first impression, that Chatterton was simply a bookish man whose fascination was with history rather than evidence of a dark double life as a calculating killer. Suddenly, Blizzard felt strangely out of place but, having been challenged to ask his questions, he had to say something.

'I am just interested,' he began, 'if any of you have any ideas about who might be behind the strange appearance of the Vengeance Man? Anyone outside your organization who may have expressed, shall we say, an unhealthy interest in the story of John Ignatius White?'

It was a question to which he expected no useful reply but at least it was something.

'You're John Blizzard, aren't you?' asked a somewhat stately man in his seventies, standing up and approaching the chief inspector. 'I recognized you from the picture in the newspaper.'

'Yes I am. And you are?'

The man, a slightly stooped individual with a neatly-cropped white moustache and twinkling blue eyes, held out a hand.

'I have always wanted to meet you,' he said in his educated voice, 'I am Albert Prendergast....'

'The Albert Prendergast?' asked Blizzard, stepping forward and shaking the hand enthusiastically. The old man's grip was firm, belying his age.

'Well, an Albert Prendergast,' said the man with a gentle smile.

'I had no idea you lived around here. I thought you lived out Sheffield way.'

'I have only just moved to the area,' said Prendergast, whose book on steam locomotives, including its section on the Silver Flyer, was regarded with deep respect by the members of the railway society of which Blizzard was such a prominent member. 'My wife died some months ago and I came here to be closer to my son and his boy. Daniel. Lovely lad. David runs his own business up here now. He and Daniel moved here from Lincolnshire.'

'I'm from Lincolnshire,' smiled Blizzard.

'Perhaps,' ventured Chatterton, seizing the moment, 'since our speaker has cried off, you and Albert might like to spare us some time to talk about steam locomotives, Mr Blizzard?'

'Well, I am rather busy....' began Blizzard.

But a look at the eager faces changed his mind as did the

chance to discuss steam locomotives with like-minded people. There were not many around – the reaction within police circles tended to vary between head-tapping indulgence to sniggering behind his back – so it was a golden opportunity. For the next hour and a half – he did not know where the time went – Blizzard spoke about his beloved project, answering their many questions and regularly demurring to allow Albert Prendergast to interject with his thoughts. At one point the chief inspector even took a call from Colley on his mobile phone and informed the bemused sergeant that he was on the right track in a very delicate inquiry and would have to get back to him. This brought appreciative smiles from the society members.

It was only towards the end of the meeting that Blizzard was able to drag himself reluctantly back to the subject in hand.

'This has been fascinating,' he said, meaning every word, 'and I thank you for the opportunity to talk about our work on the Old Lady but I do need to ask some questions of my own, gentlemen.'

'Of course,' nodded Chatterton. 'Forgive us, Chief Inspector. We rather forgot ourselves. I think I can say with some confidence that the reason the members here know about John White is that I have....'

And he smiled.

'... how can I say it? Bored them with it over recent weeks.'

'That's not true,' said the businessman speaking for the first time. 'It has been most illuminating.'

'Sorry, and your name is?' asked Blizzard.

'Robert Stanshall.'

'Of course,' said Blizzard, suddenly recalling where he had seen the man before.

Robert Stanshall's face had been in the papers many times when he proposed a £50m redevelopment of an old airfield and a huge swathe of surrounding farmland on the south side of the river, the central plank of which was a huge theme park the likes of which the area had never seen. The idea had courted controversy right from the start. Covering fifty acres, the initial plans for its rides, ever larger and more spectacular, had brought about great fury in the neighbouring well-to-do villages, whose residents were worried about traffic congestion and ruined Sunday afternoons and had protested to the council in great numbers. The local Conservative MP even spoke out against the plan.

The council turned the scheme down but Stanshall, belligerent and bullish as ever, had gone to appeal and won. Now the theme park had been open for several months, having come through its first summer season, and the villagers were living with the reality of their worst fears, roads clogged up by cars and loud music blaring out throughout the day. Stanshall had dismissed their complaints and pointed to the hundreds of jobs his venture had created in a rural employment blackspot.

'You've ruffled a few feathers,' observed Blizzard.

'And you haven't in your time?' asked Stanshall shrewdly.

'Point taken,' said Blizzard, turning to the rest of them. 'Anyway, what I need to know is if anyone outside this group is likely to know much about John Ignatius White?'

They shook their heads.

'It is a fascinating scenario, however,' ventured one of the members.

'Indeed,' nodded another, 'there certainly are some strange parallels with the incidents surrounding White, particularly if you examine the work of Adam Prior, written I believe, Bob, just three years after the death of John Ignatius?'

'Yes, indeed,' agreed Chatterton, rooting round in his bag for a document. 'What is more fascinating is the way that whoever is presenting themselves as a modern day John Ignatius White has clearly taken note of the allusions noted in the follow up book by James Bartholomew, published in seventeen hundred. I have a photocopy of the salient passages if anyone wishes to borrow it. And if you take it against the backdrop of events in Cromwell's Protectorate, with its renewed Puritanism, you can clearly see that....'

As the discussion gathered pace, Blizzard made his excuses and left them. No one seemed to really notice that he had gone. It was only when he got to the front gate of the school that he realized what was troubling him; a teenager was lying cold on a mortuary slab and there they were debating the incident as if he was a question in a history examination. And for some reason he could not fathom, the presence of a man such as Robert Stanshall in such incongruous surroundings, had disturbed Blizzard as well. Driving back to Abbey Road Police Station, Blizzard felt a deep sense of foreboding that something was very wrong behind the respectable façade of modern-day Heston village.

CHAPTER **ELEVEN**

The main hall at Heston Comprehensive School was packed that night with more than three hundred people seated on rows of chairs and a further fifty or so standing around the edge of the room. What was striking about the gathering was that, angry or not, these were no militant anti-police protestors seizing on the events in the village to make trouble, rather honest, upstanding citizens increasingly alarmed at the disintegration of law and order in their area. They were well-to-do professional people, doctors, accountants, teachers, council officers, law-abiding men and women, many of them parents of children at the school and all prepared to turn out on a wet and windy winter evening to demand action from a police force for which they instinctively had the utmost of respect most of the time. Indeed, a number of them were Neighbourhood Watch volunteers and one or two had served on police forums.

Sitting on the raised stage at the front, Ronald and Blizzard scanned the rows for some familiar faces. Ronald noticed one or two members of his Rotary Club and the two local Conservative councillors, Blizzard recognized several of the teachers from the comprehensive, John Pendrie among them, and a number of historical society members but not, he noted with interest, Bob Chatterton. There was also Marty Cundall, dressed in fatigues as usual and sitting in animated conversation with several parents. Occasionally they glanced at the stage as Marty nodded at the officers and made a particularly telling point. Over in one corner were a number of local shopkeepers, all visibly angry at what they saw as a failure to protect their properties from robbery.

Blizzard sighed; he detested this kind of event at the best of times, and this was definitely not the best of times. And he knew what was about to come. He had been given a taster when he and Colley were involved in some inquiries in the village that afternoon and within five minutes, and independent of each other, three people had approached them in the market-place to complain. One was a pensioner who said she was scared to go out – Blizzard resisted the temptation to ask her what she was doing in the village then. The second was a mother with a teenage child at the school; she was worried about the availability of drugs at the school gates. The third was a middle-aged man with a dog, who said he was concerned at the spate of burglaries in the village which, he presumed, were carried out by drug users. He said the usual obligatory things about things not being like that in his day. It was all rubbish, of course, thought Blizzard, history always wore rose-tinted spectacles. The chief inspector had replied to them with the usual placatory words but each conversation only served to strengthen his determination to put things right, whoever it upset.

Now, he glanced down at his hurriedly scribbled notes and hoped that the statistics about falling overall crime in Heston over the past two years would assuage the sense of restrained outrage that he sensed in the atmosphere and on the audience's faces. If he were a resident, he reflected glumly, it would do no such thing.

What made Blizzard's mood worse was that Chief Superintendent Bond had insisted, after an earlier sharp exchange of words with Arthur Ronald, that he chair the meeting and now sat, staunch and puffed-up with self-importance, in the middle of the two detectives, Blizzard expressionless on one side and a fuming Ronald on the other. Bond, a bulky man in his early fifties, with fleshy cheeks, florid features and peppery-coloured thinning hair, had once been a reasonable individual, in Blizzard's view, a down-to-earth bobby who knew what the job entailed. But having been singled out for career progression and being sent on numerous training courses, he had turned into one of those police officers who the chief inspector detested, all pips and jargon. Bond, who knew exactly how Blizzard felt about him – because the chief inspector once told him – had glowered at the detective when he arrived at the school and had declined to speak to him since. Which suited Blizzard fine. It also suited Ronald who, ever the diplomat, had made a feeble effort to keep the peace between the two men but had soon given up, neither officer having shown even the remotest inclination to improve their frosty relationship.

Now, having shuffled his notes ostentatiously, Bond stood up, surveyed the gathering solemnly and cleared his throat in a way that suggested he was about to say something of great import. All eyes were fixed expectantly on him and Blizzard could sense the superintendent's satisfaction at the impact he was having.

'Ladies and gentlemen,' he said as the murmuring died down, 'I appreciate this opportunity to address this gathering and to elucidate some of the ongoing strategic policing and community safety issues that the divisional command team in the southern area has implemented over recent....'

'In English, fatso!' shouted a voice.

Blizzard, stifling a smirk and noticing Colley grinning as he leaned against a wall at the back of the hall, scanned the faces in the audience to see who had shouted out. Marty Cundall caught his eye and winked.

'There is no need to let this get personal,' blustered Bond. 'The police deserve more respect....'

'Respect is earned not given,' said a man down the front.

Blizzard nodded instinctively.

'Indeed,' said Bond, uncomfortably aware that he was already losing control of the situation and equally aware that Blizzard appeared to be enjoying the spectacle, 'and we are doing everything within our power to resolve this situation.'

'But you're not, are you?' said a voice and Robert Stanshall stood up. 'This has been a police balls-up from start to finish.'

There were murmurings of agreement and a ripple of applause ran round the room. Blizzard studied Stanshall with interest. Like the first time they had met earlier in the day, he could see that there was something magnetic about him. Stanshall was one of those people who drew the eye to him and Blizzard sensed the deference of the people around him as they waited for his next utterance. It seemed that Stanshall had become their unofficial spokesman.

'This has not been a police balls-up as you so crudely describe it,' said Bond angrily.

'Maybe it's an ongoing strategic police balls-up!' shouted Cundall crudely and there was a lot of laughter.

Blizzard smiled, a small gesture but large enough to be noticed by the infuriated Bond, who glared down at him. The chief inspector stopped smiling but the damage was done. Before Bond could say anything else, Stanshall was speaking again and everyone was listening to his words, spoken as they were in the forceful and passionate way that characterized the way he lived his life and conducted his business, defying the superintendent to deny the truth of what he said.

'You see, I have a very personal interest in this, Mr Bond,' said Stanshall. 'My son was at Heston Comprehensive eighteen months ago until I took him out and enrolled him in a private school. And the reason, Mr Bond? He was being offered heroin. The school did nothing about it then and from what I hear, the police are doing nothing about it now. And now you have parents frightened to let their children out at night because some lunatic is running around murdering them. Hardly the kind of situation likely to reassure the public, which is what I assume your tortured sentences are designed to do.'

'Mr Stanshall,' said Bond, desperately trying to compete with the businessman, who now eyed him keenly. 'I appreciate your misgivings but I can assure you that in the district policing strategy to which I referred earlier, drug abuse has a very high priority, which translates itself into additional on-the-ground resourcing when we come to allocate our strategic policing funds.'

'For God's sake,' murmured Blizzard and received another glare from the irate superintendent, who seemed momentarily lost for words.

Stanshall was not.

'With due respect,' he said in a voice which suggested no due respect at all, 'you're spouting jargon without actually telling us anything, Mr Bond. Were this Barton lad and his cronies ever charged with any offences?'

'Well,' began Bond uncomfortably, 'there were some ongoing intelligence-led inquiries into the operations of a small group of....'

'Were they ever charged?' insisted Stanshall.

'Like I said, there were....' floundered Bond.

'Were they ever charged?' asked Stanshall, the third time he had asked the question, a fact not lost on the audience among which the ugly murmurings had started up again.

'No they were not,' admitted Bond, 'but that does not....'

'Why were they not charged?' asked Stanshall.

'Yeah!' shouted Cundall, leaping angrily to his feet as there were shouts from the audience. 'Why not? Why are you not protecting our children?'

'Well ... I er....' stammered Bond, taken aback by the ferocity of the attack and realizing as a flashgun went off that a reporter and photographer from the evening paper had slipped into the room. The reporter was scribbling furiously; he knew the next day's front page lead when he saw it. This time it was Ronald's time to smile. Being humiliated on the front page of the evening paper tended not to play well with those who selected assistant chief constables.

'At least the Vengeance Man gets the scum off the streets,' shouted another man.

'And *he* does something about the drug dealers,' said a smartly-dressed middle-aged woman pointedly, standing to her feet, her anger barely repressed. 'Which is more than you woodentops do.'

The insult seemed incongruous coming from her lips and there was a smattering of applause. Blizzard pursed his lips. It was just the kind of reaction he had been fearing.

'And what about these armed robbers?' shouted another man, standing up and jabbing a finger at Bond. 'What have you done about them?'

Blizzard looked at him with interest. He had never met him but, as with Stanshall, he recognized him from his picture in the newspaper. This was Derek Stoddart, the vigorous chairman of the Heston and District Association of Shopkeepers. Aged in his mid-fifties, lean and fit with greying hair and an increasingly lined face with sunken eyes, which made him look older than he was, Stoddart had been the first of the shopkeepers to be robbed by the gang.

They had burst into one of his shops on one of the estates bordering Heston a few weeks before and threatened his wife before snatching money from her and smashing the front window with the butt of a gun as they fled. The incident had enraged and upset Stoddart and had left his wife deeply traumatized, so much so that she had been unable to work since and suffered what doctors said was a mild stroke a few days after the incident. She was now a semi-invalid and Stoddart wanted someone to blame. Bond was an easy target.

Blizzard knew about Stoddart because the shopkeeper had been increasingly voluble in the local media about the robberies, citing the massive impact it had had on himself and his family and suggesting that the police should be doing more to catch the perpetrators. He had been involved in several stormy meetings with Superintendent Bond at Abbey Road Police Station and had also confronted him at a public police forum, each time repeatedly demanding a greater police presence on the streets. Each time, Bond had rejected the call, citing financial resources, further enraging Stoddart who made some hard-hitting comments to the media. When they read the resultant negative coverage in the evening newspaper, and Bond's jargon-filled responses, Blizzard and Ronald had groaned, dismayed at the impression it gave of a police force losing control and not particularly dedicated to the protection of the people living and working in its area.

Blizzard could understand Stoddart's anger at the uniform presence but felt more comfortable with CID's role in the matter. The chief inspector knew how many hours his team under Ramsey had put into the inquiry and how frustrated they were at the lack of a breakthrough. Blizzard and Ramsey had spoken about the situation many times since the death of Eddie Barton and had both supported the theory that his gang was behind the armed robberies, a belief strengthened by the fact that there had been no more raids since the murder. Blizzard had even gone as far as to predict that the gang was running scared and that there would not be any more robberies until the Vengeance Man was behind bars. The moment he said it, an image of someone counting chickens flashed into his mind but it was too late then. The words had come out.

'You've done nowt about it,' shouted Stoddart furiously, advancing down the central aisle towards the startled Superintendent Bond, who had never seen him this angry.

'Allow me to answer that one,' said Ronald suddenly standing up, having lost patience with his blustering colleague.

Gesturing to the astonished Bond to sit down, to ironic cheers from the audience, Ronald said, 'I think there are two issues here. On the robberies, I can understand the shopkeepers' frustration but I believe that from the CID point of view we have done all that we could have done to catch them....'

There were mutterings from some of the shop owners.

'Typical,' snorted a man, 'you always defend your own.'

'Hear me out,' said Ronald, holding up a hand.

The room fell silent, the audience sensing an authority in Ronald's tone of voice, which they had not detected in the floundering Superintendent Bond.

Ronald used the seconds as the hubbub died down to do some rapid thinking.

'Clearly,' he said, 'we have not yet succeeded in our job because they are not in custody yet. However, without giving too much away, I can say that we have made significant progress in the inquiry and may be close to identifying them.'

An excited murmur ran round the room. There had been a definite change in the mood of the audience as they sensed that here was a police officer able to speak to them in terms they could understand. Yes, they were still angry but there was something about Arthur Ronald that persuaded them to hear him out. However, they would be wrong to underestimate him and assume that his amiable bearing denoted a man who was prepared to fall on his sword without argument. Ronald was about to turn the tables on them.

'Moving on to the drug dealers,' continued Ronald. 'There have indeed been pronounced failings in the way this affair has been dealt with by the police. Myself and Superintendent Bond have been discussing this today, as a matter of fact, and we, as a force, must hold our hands up to our failings.'

Bond stared at him in amazement and seemed about to speak when a sharp look from Ronald silenced him.

'However,' said Ronald, 'it would be wrong to simply blame the police....'

He held up a hand as a few members of the audience shouted out, raising his voice to regain the initiative.

'Let me finish, please. You can make your points in a moment or two. You asked a question, Mr Stanshall, and I am endeavouring to answer it.'

'Let him speak,' said Stanshall, his reply causing the uproar to die down.

Blizzard noticed that Bond was starting to struggle to his feet again so the chief inspector tugged gently on his jacket sleeve and shook his head as the humiliated superintendent stared down at him.

'Let Arthur handle this,' said Blizzard quietly. 'He speaks English.'

Bond seemed about to respond but thought better of it and sat back down, sitting biting his lip furiously as Ronald continued his address.

'There is a community responsibility in all of this,' said Ronald, pausing to let the words sink in and deliberately scanning the room slowly, secretly enjoying the dramatic effect as some of those who had shouted loudest refused to meet his gaze. 'And what do I mean by that? Well, how many of you knew about what was happening here...?'

A forest of hands went up, some more tentatively than others but raised all the same. As he paused for effect, one or two more were raised.

'And how many of you came forward to tell the police that you would testify against the dealers? '

There was silence.

'Exactly. Even you, Mr Stanshall,' said Ronald evenly, looking at the businessman. 'Did you contact the police when your son was offered drugs?'

'I told the school,' said Stanshall, sounding defensive for the first time.

He was not used to being out-manoeuvred.

'Hardly an answer,' said Ronald, deliberately adopting the technique of repeating the same question that Stanshall had used so effectively against Bond a few moments ago. 'So, I ask again, did you tell the police?'

'I assumed....'

'We could achieve so much more if that word could be removed from the English language. There has been far too much assuming round here,' replied Ronald and looked directly at Marty Cundall. 'And you, yes, you Mr Cundall, you were angry about drugs being offered to your son. Quite rightly. But I have been doing some checking. When your son was offered drugs you stormed into Heston Police Station and demanded that Constable Fearnley arrest the dealers. However, when he asked if you would sign a statement identifying Eddie Barton you refused, did you not?'

Cundall gaped at him, mouth hanging open, astonished and embarrassed by the revelation and acutely aware that every eye in the hall was on him.

'Well?' asked Ronald.

'I ain't a writing kind of man,' mumbled Cundall at length.

'Indeed,' said Ronald as laughter trickled round the room. 'And like it or not, we are not the kind of people to go round charging people without the evidence to back it up. And yes....'

He held up his hand again as a few people started muttering.

'Yes, I know we have not acquitted ourselves particularly well here but you have a responsibility as well. We want these people, we want them really badly. Drugs are a scourge and have no place in Heston....'

There was a ripple of applause. This was what people wanted to hear.

'But we cannot do it on our own. If we had taken what little real evidence we had on these dealers to the Crown Prosecution Service, they would have told us to find more. Ladies and gentlemen, if you can finger the drug dealers come and tell us. Yes, I know they can be intimidating, yes I know they can be frightening, but if people do not stand up against them, they will wreck this village and none of us wants that.'

Murmurs of agreement.

'DCI Blizzard here,' and Ronald nodded to the chief inspector, 'has assumed overall control of our investigation into the murder of Eddie Barton and the robberies but he cannot do it on his own. He may think he is, but he is not Superman. And he wears his underpants under his trousers.'

It was a gentle joke, meant in friendship rather than maliciously, and one that elicited a few chuckles around the room as well as bringing a smile out of John Blizzard. Billy Bond merely continued to fume as he sat, arms crossed, and glared balefully at the ceiling.

'We are in this together, whether you like it or not,' continued Ronald. 'We are convinced that people out there – maybe even in this hall – know more than they are letting on. We have been met with a wall of silence. It is time, ladies and gentlemen, to start removing the bricks.'

And he sat down, leaving his final words hanging in the air as a challenge to the audience. Surreptitiously slipping his scribbled crime figures back into his jacket pocket, Blizzard glanced across and nodded his appreciation at Ronald. The chief superintendent gave the merest of smiles then turned to the acutely embarrassed Billy Bond. The journalist scribbled furiously. Front page lead and an inside spread with a huge *Special Report by* ... he was thinking.

'Now,' said Ronald, nodding at Bond, 'The superintendent here will tell you about the increased patrols he this afternoon authorised in Heston in order to crack down on street dealing, won't you? And I expect that you afford him a greater degree of respect than you did earlier.'

And he beamed at the deflated superintendent.

'That man,' murmured Ramsey, who had slipped into the room midway through Ronald's speech and was now standing next to Colley, 'will be a chief constable yet.'

'Na,' said Colley drily, 'Have you seen his golf swing…?'

CHAPTER **TWELVE**

Saturday saw the police continuing their vigorous public reassurance campaign in Heston with Arthur Ronald seizing the initiative from the hapless, and increasingly sidelined, Billy Bond. After they left the meeting at the school the night before, Bond had let loose a volley of expletives at both Ronald and Blizzard as they walked down the school path to their cars. Watched by disgusted parents, he claimed that the detectives had set out to make him look stupid in front of the packed hall. Blizzard's comment that Bond did not require help to make him look stupid hardly improved the situation and, conscious of the crowd that had gathered to witness the spectacle, the superintendent and Ronald agreed to meet the following morning at Abbey Road Police Station to thrash things out.

Things did not go according to plan for Bond because when the first edition of the evening paper landed on his desk, it revealed appreciation of the way Arthur Ronald dealt with the public's concerns and an editorial praising him for his honesty. Given the force's often difficult relationship with the local newspaper, it made for heartening reading and shortly after the story came out, the deputy chief constable rang Ronald and ordered that he assume charge of public relations duties in the area and that Bond's task be to ensure that there were plenty of high-profile patrols around Heston.

A furious Bond stalked off home, leaving Ronald and Blizzard to map out a plan of action. Not normally one for public relations, Blizzard threw himself into this task whole-heartedly, partly because of his belief that the force had to do much better and partly because he wanted to support Arthur Ronald. He could also see that Assistant Chief Constable Ronald had a nice ring to it, and friends in high places always came in handy. The result was that, in addition to receiving regular updates on the investigation from his officers, Blizzard also attended a series of meetings throughout the day, designed not just to provide reassurance but also to turn the heat up on those who could help. Blizzard remained convinced that too many people were withholding too much information and with plenty of people with reason to hate Barton and his cronies, it was time to increase the pressure before things got totally out of hand and the vigilante killer struck again.

The first visitor, at noon, was Robert Stanshall, sitting calm and collected in Ronald's office and eyeing the detectives coolly. A man used to dominating meetings and those around him, an interview with a couple of police officers presented few concerns for Stanshall. Nevertheless, Ronald's performance the night before had impressed him and made him wary.

'Thank you for coming in, Mr Stanshall,' said Ronald, courteous as ever. 'We appreciate your help.'

'I can hardly refuse it after that little speech of yours. I particularly liked the line about removing bricks. Very slick.'

'Thank you. So tell me, in the light of what has happened, would your son be prepared to sign a statement saying who offered to sell him the drugs?'

'He is still frightened of them,' said Stanshall, keen to be seen to be helping but also concerned about possible repercussions against his teenage son. 'They are bad lads, superintendent. Bad, bad lads.'

'They may well be,' nodded Ronald, 'but like I said last night, there is no way we can do anything unless people put their head above the parapet.'

'An unfortunate line with shopkeepers being shot,' murmured Stanshall, adding shrewdly. 'Besides, isn't that an easy get-out for you? Turn the blame back on the public to paper over the cracks?'

'I admitted our failings last night,' said Ronald. 'And I meant it. But it is also time for the public to admit its responsibilities. Some may regard it as a buzzword, but tackling crime is a partnership.'

Stanshall considered the point for a moment or two. A hard-headed businessman used to tough choices, he had seen the argument's logic the night before and he saw it now but, unlike with business, there was a personal side to all of this. For Robert Stanshall there was still the very real worry about what would happen to his son if anyone found out that he had been speaking to the police. As it stood, the challenge had been issued at the meeting but as far as anyone was concerned, Stanshall had not taken it up. He had deliberately said nothing to the press after the meeting and even his visit to the police station was done without publicity. The officers had sent an unmarked car to pick him up and had brought him in the back entrance, a gesture that had surprised a relieved and grateful Stanshall. As a result, he felt a trust in Ronald and Blizzard that he had not felt when Superintendent Bond got to his feet and started blustering the night before.

'Very well,' said Stanshall at length, prepared to repay the gesture. 'I will ask my boy to give a statement – I can only ask him, mind – and I want a guarantee that he will be protected.'

'I can't put a copper on every door,' said Ronald. 'You know that.'

'Granted – but I want to make sure that these thugs don't know it was him.'

'That is not a promise I can make,' replied Ronald. 'The statement may be read out in court – I can't pretend it won't. But the best protection we can give people like your son is to get these lads off the streets for a long time.'

'Well just make sure you do,' said Stanshall and got up
to leave, pointing a finger at the officers. 'Just make sure
you do.'

After he left, the detectives prepared for their next
meeting. So it was that, shortly after two, Derek Stoddart
could be found sipping tea in Ronald's office, skilfully
beguiled by the detectives' respectful approach into
assuming that he was the one in control of the situation. It
was part of the detectives' strategy to wrong-foot him but
as the meeting started, Derek Stoddart suspected nothing.
Sitting eyeing the detectives he felt confident. Stoddart
was a pompous self-important individual, the kind of
person who, like Stanshall, was used to being in charge of
a situation. And he felt in charge now. Although he
thought Blizzard looked a bit of a tough cookie, he was
reassured by Ronald's avuncular appearance, almost like a
much-loved uncle, and saw no reason to mistrust his
motives. Ronald was not about to disavow him – at least
not at first.

'I appreciate you coming in for this chat,' began Ronald.
'Of course, everything said within these walls is confidential. I am sure you appreciate that. But we do need your
help, Mr Stoddart.'

Stoddart puffed out his chest. This was the kind of thing
he could understand all too easily. Proof that he was an
important member of the community, someone to be
trusted with delicate information, someone to confide in.

'Yes, well, always happy to help,' said Stoddart.
'Particularly since I don't have to talk to that half-wit
Bond.'

'You must not judge him too harshly,' said Ronald diplo-
matically. 'He is a good officer is Superintendent Bond.'

'I appreciate the loyalty,' said Stoddart gruffly, 'but
people like me and my members need to see action and not
just words. Too many of my members are terrified of these
thugs and it's getting more and more difficult to find new
staff. You said in the meeting that you were gleaning useful

information about the robbers. Are you able to tell me anything more?'

'As long as it does not go outside these four walls,' nodded Ronald, leaning forward conspiratorially as he laid his trap. 'I assume we can trust you with highly confidential information?'

'You can.'

This was the kind of talk Stoddart liked. Blizzard sat back and watched the spider spin the web about its prey.

'Our information,' said Ronald in a low voice, 'is that Eddie Barton and his associates committed the robberies.'

'Thought as much,' said Stoddart.

'Come again?' asked Ronald.

'Nothing,' mumbled Stoddart, angry for letting the comment slip out.

'It didn't sound like nothing to me.'

'OK,' sighed Stoddart. 'You were right in that meeting. People do know more than they have been letting on.'

'Go on.'

'After the last robbery, the one where poor Harry was shot, I was approached by one of my customers. He said that a few weeks ago, he saw Eddie Barton and Roger Colclough on the wasteland near Heston Rec. They were with a man and my customer thought he saw a shotgun. He got the impression they were buying it from him.'

'Jesus Christ!' exclaimed Blizzard. 'How come this person didn't come and tell us? It would have saved an awful lot of trouble!'

'I did tell him that but this person knows Colclough's mother very well. It put him in a difficult situation. I am sure you can appreciate that.'

'Not as difficult as the shopkeeper who was shot. One of your members, for God's sake!' exclaimed Blizzard. 'And what about your wife? How difficult do things have to get for her before you and your people co-operate with us?'

'I know,' mumbled Stoddart, realizing he had made a huge tactical error. 'But he knows what Roger Colclough is like. He was agonizing for weeks over this but you were right, Mr Ronald, people are terrified of them.'

'Yes, but we can't do anything about them unless we are given this kind of information,' pointed out the exasperated chief inspector.

'I can see the argument and I am great supporter of the police – of course, I am – but not everyone would see it that way....' and Stoddart paused.

The detectives eyed him keenly. Something about the way he had stopped talking so abruptly and was now looking at them nervously had alerted their curiosity. It was nearly time to reveal their hand to the good Mr Stoddart, part of their policy of not just addressing public concerns but also re-establishing police control.

'Perhaps you would like to elaborate on that comment?' said Blizzard.

'I can't.'

The voice was defensive. Evasive.

'Mr Stoddart,' said Blizzard, 'Last night, the chief superintendent here appealed for help sorting this out. If you know something....'

'I don't know anything about Colclough or the others,' said the shopkeeper quickly.

'Then perhaps there is something else you might want to tell us,' replied Blizzard, eyeing him keenly.

'Not really. No. It was a poor choice of words....'

'Actually, I think it was the right choice of words,' replied Blizzard. 'Let me help you with your dilemma. Tell me about your chat with Marty Cundall please, Mr Stoddart.'

'What do you mean?'

The answer was supposed to sound casual, unconcerned, but the tone of voice and the evasive movements suggested it was anything but. Derek Stoddart was a worried man and the beads of sweat glistened on his forehead.

'According to my sergeant, you seemed to be getting

quite animated when you and some of your members talked to him after the meeting.'

'Animated like you and Superintendent Bond?' asked Stoddart wickedly.

'Don't change the subject. What were you talking to Marty about?'

'I don't have to tell you. I can talk to whom I like about what I like. It's a free world.'

'Indeed it is. And because it is a free world, we invited our Mr Cundall to have a nice little chat with us down the station this morning....'

'Oh, God,' breathed Stoddart.

'And, do you know what, it turns out you were not discussing the cost of a loaf of bread after all. Do you know what he told us, Mr Stoddart?'

'Yes.'

The voice was little more than a croak.

'I do not think I have to remind you,' said Ronald, taking over as the chief inspector sat back in his chair and enjoyed the effect his words had had on the shopkeeper, 'that taking the law into your hands is illegal.'

'We wouldn't do anything like that,' protested Stoddart but it did not sound convincing.

'What did he offer?'

A pause.

'Mr Stoddart,' said Blizzard and the shopkeeper was acutely aware, as many a villain had been down the years, of the chief inspector's ice-blue eyes focused on him.

'OK,' he said at length. 'OK. Marty Cundall said that he would arrange some protection for the shops....'

'Protection?'

'Ask around, try to track down the guys who were doing the robberies,' explained Stoddart. 'Get some of his friends to keep an eye on the businesses.'

'I take it you know what Marty Cundall's friends are like?' said Blizzard.

'I told him it was a bad idea,' said Stoddart uncomfortably.

'And your colleagues agreed with you?' asked Blizzard.

'Most of them.'

'But not all of them?'

'Not all of them,' nodded Stoddart miserably, adding hurriedly, 'but I am sure they would not really have taken him up on his offer. That's not the way our members do things, Mr Blizzard. We respect the law.'

'I accept most of you wouldn't countenance such a thing but there's a couple of your members who are not exactly pillars of the community, are they? That shop off Renfrew Street, for example, I don't imagine he gets down to Rotary all that often. Probably burgled half of them.'

'No but....'

'And I seem to recall Detective Inspector Ramsey lifting the one on Barlow Street for selling stolen video recorders under the counter last year.'

Stoddart sat back weakly – this was not going the way he had envisaged when he was summonsed to see the officers. He had viewed it as a form of victory, confirmation of his influence in the Western area, something to strengthen his position as leader of the Heston and District Association of Shopkeepers, something to impress his members and emphasize his authority at a time when many of them were questioning so much in their lives, something to crow about in the media. It might even, he thought hopefully, prove a launch-pad for a place on the council at the next election. But for now, he was finding things distinctly less comfortable and could feel Blizzard's eyes boring into him again. Suddenly, Stoddart had visions of this little unpleasantness leaking to the media and of the disaster that would be for his political aspirations. And he realized how effectively and easily he had been out-manoeuvred.

'I would suggest,' said Ronald, taking advantage of the impact the chief inspector's steely gaze was having, 'that you tell your members not to even consider Mr Cundall's generous offer. I take it we have an agreement?'

Stoddart nodded feebly at them and, clearly dazed,

allowed Blizzard to usher him out of the room without further word. A few moments later, the chief inspector was back with a wide grin on his face.

'That went well,' said a satisfied Ronald.

'Sure did,' nodded Blizzard.

'Another cuppa?'

'No, I've got a little job to attend to.'

'Ah, yes,' said the superintendent. 'It always seems to come back to chummy, doesn't it? Have fun.'

'This is the most fun I've had all week,' beamed Blizzard.

Three minutes later he had met up with Dave Colley and together they headed for the interview room in which was Marty Cundall, dressed as usual in his army fatigues and green T-shirt. He had not shaved that morning and a thick stubble covered his chin. He looked to the detectives as if he had not washed either.

'How do you want to play it?' hissed Colley as he pushed open the door.

'I thought I'd give him some rope and let him hang himself – save us a job,' replied the chief inspector.

'Now, Marty,' he smiled affably as Cundall eyed them suspiciously. 'Where were we? Ah, that's right, tell me again about your kind offer to sort out the drug dealers for the grateful shopkeepers?'

'I ain't done nothing wrong,' protested Cundall.

'Yet,' said Blizzard pointedly, pulling up a chair. 'Listen, Marty, as it stands there are plenty of reasons for me to think that you killed Eddie Barton.'

'But I didn't!' said Cundall, suddenly looking scared.

'I think that may well be the case,' nodded Blizzard, 'but look at it from my point of view. You thump Eddie Barton then he gets killed and now I hear that you are offering protection for the shopkeepers. What am I supposed to think? You're a loose cannon, Marty, and I don't like loose cannons on my manor.'

'I only meant....' but Cundall stopped abruptly, realizing that he had to choose his words carefully. 'I only meant that

I would keep an eye on the shops for them. I have a few associates who could....'

'Big Davie Grewcock among them, I imagine,' said Colley, thinking of the huge bodybuilder who ran with Cundall.

'Listen, Marty,' said Blizzard, leaning forward and fixing him with a steely glare, 'let me make this clear. This is a difficult enough situation without some bloody Army reject careering around t....'

'Army reject!' yelled Cundall, leaping to his feet. 'Who you calling a bloody Army reject? I had an exemplary military record, Chief Inspector!'

'Two raps for assault as I recall,' said Blizzard drily. 'And there was a nasty little incident with a sergeant as well, wasn't there?'

'But he peeled a damned fine spud,' said Colley.

'I was a good soldier!' shouted Cundall. 'In the Army I was an exemplary....'

'Yes, well, you're not in the Army now,' snapped Blizzard. 'You play by my rules now so sit down and shut up.'

Cundall eyed him for a moment but one look into those ice-blue eyes was enough and he sat down heavily.

'Thank you – now let me make this clear,' said Blizzard. 'You have already admitted attacking Eddie Barton. Scumbag or not, it's still a crime. I'll let the CPS work out what to do now he's dead. As it stands, you haven't done anything illegal with the shopkeepers but if I hear so much as a whisper that you have started anything, I warn you, I'll be down on you like a ton of bricks. Do I make myself clear?'

Cundall nodded meekly. John Blizzard was known throughout the criminal world in Hafton and everyone who had crossed him knew that he delivered on his promises. There were plenty of villains behind the bars of Hafton Prison who would testify to that and Cundall had no desire to join them.

'Good,' said Blizzard, leaning back in his chair. 'Because, frankly Marty, I have had about as much as I can take today … and you know what a foul temper I have.'

Blizzard beamed. Marty Cundall looked miserably at the floor. It had not been a good day, all in all.

CHAPTER **THIRTEEN**

Any sense of satisfaction John Blizzard might have been experiencing after the day's events was rudely shattered by the phone call that shook him roughly from sleep shortly after one that Sunday morning, heralding the end of the search for Roger Colclough. Blizzard should have known better; in his experience with complex investigations like this, every time he allowed himself to think things were going well, something happened to bring him back down to earth.

He had, however, been allowed a pleasant few hours away from the pressure of police work for what remained of his Saturday. Before he went home, he had a very pleasant task to do which was why, after leaving the police station having bailed Marty Cundall pending further inquiries and letting him go with a stern warning ringing in his ears, Blizzard headed out to Heston. A quarter of an hour later he parked his car outside one of the detached houses in a neat little cul-de-sac at the furthest end of one of the new estates. Noting the close-cropped lawn and the manicured weed-free borders, Blizzard rang on the front door bell.

It was opened by a man in his forties, dressed casually yet smartly in pressed cream slacks and a navy blue jumper out of which peeped a finely starched collar. Looking into the rounded face, Blizzard noted features with which he was already familiar. The hair, without even the merest hint of grey, was brown and curly, the face rounded and tanned with twinkling, friendly eyes, lacking the sickly pallor of so many in a Hafton winter, suggesting an outdoor life. It was the slightly crooked smile that confirmed the man's identity for the chief inspector.

'You must be David Prendergast,' said Blizzard.

'And you,' grinned the man, stretching out a welcoming hand, the rough skin indicating a manual worker, 'must be John.'

'It's nice to meet someone who does not call me chief inspector,' replied Blizzard, accepting the offer to enter the house. 'Or worse.'

'My father has spoken a lot about you. He says your decision to serve the police force was a sad loss to the world of railways,' smiled David as he led the way down the neat hall. 'Says you should be running a preservation line instead.'

'Coming from your dad,' said Blizzard, walking into the living room and sitting down in the comfy beige armchair indicated, 'that is a compliment. And although the idea does appeal sometimes, I fear it would not be a suitable life for me – not enough excitement, I am afraid.'

David Prendergast fixed him with a quizzical look.

'You like people murdering each other?' he asked.

'If people were nice to each other. I'd be out of a job.'

'That's one way of looking at it.'

'Sorry,' said Blizzard. 'Badly phrased. What I meant to say is that someone has to investigate murders and it might as well be me. I am one of those people who needs their hours to be filled or else their mind starts wandering into dangerous areas. Being a copper does that to you.'

'I am sure it does. Tea?' asked David and disappeared to busy himself in the kitchen from which the chief inspector could hear the clinking of cups and saucers.

Glancing round the room, he noted the rare railway prints – originals if he was not mistaken – and seconds later, Albert Prendergast appeared at the door, beaming as he noticed the chief inspector's admiring gaze.

'Delightful are they not?' said Albert. 'Cost me an arm and a leg.'

'But worth every penny,' said Blizzard with approval, standing up and shaking the older man's hand. 'Thank you for doing this for me.'

'No problem,' said Prendergast and reached behind the sofa to bring out several weighty books. 'Always glad to help. Like I said last time we met, I am not sure if they have the information you want but you are welcome to borrow them for as long as you want.'

'It's a close-up photograph of the Silver Flyer's cab I am really after,' said Blizzard, accepting the books gratefully. 'Some of the brackets are missing and we want to find out what type they used.'

'I am not sure you will find the information you seek in there but you are welcome to look,' said Prendergast, sitting down in the other armchair.

David bustled into the room and for the next hour or so, the three sat and chatted about anything but railways because it quickly became clear that the son did not share the father's passion for steam.

'I am afraid I have to disappoint you,' David said with a smile. 'I went into landscape gardening instead. A great let-down for dad.'

Father and son exchanged smiles. The chief inspector found himself appreciating David's easy, self-deprecating manner and the way he had selflessly agreed to let Albert live with them following his wife's death. When the chief inspector ventured as such, David said the arrangement suited everyone. His own wife had died of cancer some years before, David explained while refilling the tea cups, and to have Albert there was good company for son and teenage grandson. His father, said David, had been seeking to move into a sheltered housing scheme but nobody was particularly desperate to see it happen anytime soon. They had not seen much of Daniel while they talked but he did appear at one point, a curly haired young man dressed in sweatshirt and jeans, ambling down to make himself a sandwich before disappearing back into his room. They heard his door close and the dull thump of music started up.

It was pleasant, thought Blizzard as he walked into the misty darkness of a winter's evening more than a hour and a half later, not quite sure where the time had gone, to meet people who were not in the police and spoke of normal things.

For all his reputation for hard work, John Blizzard realized the need for all officers to get away from the pressures of the job, which was why he had accepted Ronald's invitation to his home for dinner that night. After popping home to take a shower and change out of his suit into black trousers and a dark blue shirt, Blizzard arrived at the house shortly after seven thirty. A legacy of years in the force had made Ronald extremely security-conscious – virtually ever copper Blizzard had ever known was – and the superintendent lived in a large detached house in a secure housing complex on the edge of the city, the electronically controlled gates designed to keep wrongdoers away and the house protected by surveillance cameras. 'I know where you live' might usually be an empty threat from villains but the possibility of it turning out to be true remained a police officer's biggest nightmare nevertheless.

Sitting in the spacious living room with its antique furniture, classy ornaments and high quality prints, the trappings of success for a well-paid superintendent, Blizzard enjoyed a couple of glasses of red wine then a meal cooked by Ronald's wife; she had prepared pasta knowing Blizzard's love of Italian food. The evening had been accompanied by pleasant conversation, none of it anything to do with police, and the chief inspector had headed home shortly after eleven, gone to bed, feeling suddenly weary, and had fallen asleep over his book with the light on.

It was still on when the phone call came through and,

struggling to get his bearings for a moment, Blizzard scrabbled around for the bedside phone, cursing as he knocked the receiver on to the floor.

'Blizzard,' he mumbled after recovering it and realizing he had it the wrong way round.

'It's Chris.'

'This had better be good,' mumbled Blizzard to his DI, turning the receiver round and glancing at his bedside clock.

'Not the word I would use, guv.'

The voice was flat.

'You had better get down to Heston churchyard.'

Which was why, twenty minutes later and now very much awake, John Blizzard stood with Ramsey a few yards into the graveyard, collars turned up against the foggy night chill, staring in horrified silence at the body of Roger Colclough. The teenager, clearly visible in the orange glow of the nearby streetlights, had been deliberately propped up against a gravestone, blood dribbling from his mouth and eyes rolled into the top of his head, the cause of death the metal spiked fence railing that had been thrust savagely into his back. It had penetrated him with such force that the tip was protruding through his stomach, the crimson bloodstain gradually spreading across his windcheater. In the orange glow of the street lights, it made for a grotesque scene and each of the detectives, although well used to seeing dead bodies after years in the job, had to pause for a moment to gather their thoughts and steady their stomachs.

The teenager had been discovered after an early morning patrol car spotted the Vengeance Man loping across the market-place. The two officers had given chase on foot but the stranger started running and vanished down a side alley. Convinced they had him trapped, the constables had followed only to find the alleyway empty. Baffled and a little scared, they had immediately called Ramsey, who had rushed to the village and, acting on a hunch, headed straight for the graveyard where he found the body of Roger Colclough.

'What do you reckon?' asked the DI at length.

'I think I want Marty Cundall arresting,' said Blizzard grimly.

'Surely he would not be that stupid...?' began Ramsey.

'Possibly not but the fact remains that we released him yesterday and lo and behold, we find laughing boy here.'

'Point taken,' nodded the DI.

'I take it no one else saw the Vengeance Man?'

'Just the lads,' and Ramsey nodded to the constables, who were standing at a respectful distance, trying not to look at the corpse but nevertheless finding their eyes drawn to the grisly sight.

As Blizzard walked over to them, David Colley emerged from the gloom of the graveyard, looking grim with a face illuminated eerily in his torch beam.

'Anything?' asked the chief inspector.

'Ninety seven dead bodies,' replied the deadpan sergeant. 'But don't worry, someone has kindly buried them for us.'

Blizzard gave him a withering look but for all the bleak situation, it was a good humoured one. The chief inspector had long valued the sergeant's ability to relieve tension, something that was beyond the earnest and humourless Ramsey.

'Tell me what you saw,' said Blizzard, walking back towards the entrance and addressing the uniform constables.

'We were driving through the market-place,' said the older of the two, averting his gaze from the body, 'when we saw this guy with a long black coat and a wide-brimmed hat striding past the hairdressers. He turned round and saw us and that was when he legged it.'

'Did you get a look at his face?' asked Colley.

'What face?' asked the officer.

'He didn't look like he had one,' nodded the younger constable.

'Don't you start!' snapped Blizzard, determined to stamp on any kind of talk that made officers forget they were dealing with a human being rather than someone from the realm of the undead. 'Then what happened?'

'Well, it was funny,' said the older constable. 'He stopped and stared at us as we were running towards him. It was like he wanted us to see that he wasn't afraid of us.'

'Then what?'

'He ran into the back alley next to the bakery. We followed but,' and the constable shook his head, 'he had gone. Just vanished into thin air.'

'For God's sake!' exclaimed Blizzard. 'Can we stop talking like this, please?! This is not some ghost floating around like something out of the sodding *Exorcist*, this is a real man. A very real man. If you are in any doubt, take a look at our Mister Colclough over there.'

'Yeah,' nodded the constable, glancing at the impaled corpse, 'but it makes you think, guv. It really does....'

Despite himself, Blizzard had to agree. It was indeed uncanny and he needed to find some answers quickly before all the good work of the public meeting at the school was undone. With a shake of the head, he took another look at Colclough then peered into the darkness of the graveyard with its dancing shadows. As the rain started to fall a light breeze blew up and the trees rustled. Blizzard shivered and headed for the car to wait for forensics. It was going to be a long night.

CHAPTER **FOURTEEN**

Although it was a Sunday, Abbey Road Police Station was a hive of activity the next morning. Having reviewed the inquiry with Ronald shortly after seven – following a disturbed and short sleep – Blizzard had called in officers on days off to search for the killer of Roger Colclough. The result was that, taking into account CID and uniform back-up, the chief inspector had seventy officers at his disposal that morning. His main aim was to impress on them that this was an earthly crime and not something supernatural. He had heard the mutterings and was determined to keep the investigation real. Helping that was the discovery that the Vengeance Man had not vanished into thin air the night before, rather kicked his way through a garden fence and made his escape that way. Hardly the actions of a ghost, Blizzard had said pointedly.

Shortly after eight thirty he held a briefing, telling them that the time had come to get aggressive. He wanted them, said Blizzard, to go in hard, to track down informants and lean on them, to kick underworld figures out of bed, to ask the tough questions, to, in short, put the word around that the police meant business. There was, he said sternly, to be an end to public rumblings about a police force that had lost control of the situation. If the two murdered boys were victims of some kind of drugs feud between gangland figures, he wanted to know about it.

Officers should, he said, letting his eye roam round the packed briefing room, go back to anyone with criminal connections with whom they had had dealings over the past fortnight and rattle their cages in a renewed effort to find both the missing Marty Cundall and the hide-out for the missing teenage gang members Paul Moody and Raymond Ransome. The teenagers must be shit-scared, Blizzard told them, and scared people made mistakes. Colclough had made the mistake of breaking cover and it had cost him his life, suggesting that someone was keeping a very close watch on the hideout, said the chief inspector; perhaps now the other two would cut and run as well. And if they did, Blizzard wanted them picked up, he said, his speech delivered in short staccato sentences.

This was the John Blizzard his officers liked to see, the detective who did not believe in the villains holding the initiative, the officer who was prepared to push his team hard in order to free up some tongues. And they were prepared to be pushed by him. In an age when officers were increasingly being pressed into paperwork and the need for 'community-based initiatives', a world where they heard the public complaining about a criminal justice system gone soft and where politicians drew attention to poor detection rates, here was a policeman who believed the battle could only be won on the streets. And, they could see from the pursed lips, that he was angry. Very angry.

It was a view shared by Ronald, who stood and watched, nodding his approval from time to time. He, too, had been stung by the very public criticism and was eager that people see the police respond in as high profile a manner as possible and that Abbey Road officers were reinvigorated with a renewed faith in their abilities to bring the events in Heston to a conclusion.

Ronald had another reason for wishing to see arrests; with budgets already stretched, a major investigation like this was a massive financial drain that was eating up his overtime for the year. Such was the manpower being poured into the inquiry that other crimes were being ignored. Burglaries, car thefts, assaults, the volume crime that made up the vast bulk of daily CID business in the Western Division, were being left uninvestigated. That was already leading to people living in other areas of the division complaining about the deterioration in service.

Making an arrest in the Vengeance Man case would be terrific news and renew public confidence in Heston but only until the next crime figures were published. Inevitably, being forced to ignore so much volume crime for the sake of one inquiry meant clear-up rates would drop and the statistics would again suggest a police force failing in its duty, ruining all the good work and bringing the pressure back on to Ronald, Bond and the officers under their command.

Nevertheless, for the moment Ronald was prepared to let Blizzard have the resources he needed and, as the operation got under way and early morning moved towards lunchtime, the police station was filled with a steady stream of rough-looking characters being marched into interview rooms to be questioned on what they knew about Marty Cundall. Most had crossed Blizzard during their criminal careers and he made sure they saw him standing, arms crossed, lips thin and unsmiling, when they were brought in. Turning baleful eyes on the chief inspector as they were taken for interview, they muttered curses and demanded to see their lawyers, all of which pleased him no end. Even though he knew, and they knew, it was all a game, experience had taught him that there was little honour among villains and that a heavy police onslaught would often lead them to give up one of their own just to have the heat turned off and prevent detectives discovering other secrets in their trawl.

It was a technique he had used before with great success and one he hoped would bring forth results this time. What made him uneasy was the thought that Barton and his gang – who were much younger than most of the veterans now being brought in to Abbey Road Police Station – seemed to have worked very much alone rather than as part of a network so that even villains who wanted to help the police might not know much anyway.

But there was one angle about which Blizzard was more optimistic. Although the gang had operated under its own rules, it had to buy its drugs from somewhere. To try to find out where, Abbey Road detectives had been working with their drug squad counterparts to bring in middle and low-level dealers over recent days to see what they knew. Most had stayed sullenly silent but one or two had offered some information. Another swathe of raids that morning was increasing the pressure and Blizzard was hopeful that one or two of the less experienced dealers would find themselves so spooked by the high-profile police presence that they would let something slip. Someone had to be working with the new kids on the block.

Adding to the pressure was the morning press conference hosted by Ronald and Blizzard at which they were asked some tough questions of their own about events in Heston. However, the media were clearly impressed by the officers' uncompromising talking and by the constant comings and goings of police vehicles and officers at Abbey Road and the intensive patrols in Heston, to which the shrewd Ronald had given the press photographers and television cameramen open access. Equally crucially, he had deliberately kept the hapless Billy Bond away from the media.

However, as morning slipped into afternoon, the unpalatable fact remained that two people were dead and detectives were nowhere nearer to finding out who carried out the murders. Forensic searches of the graveyard had gleaned nothing, the post mortem on Colclough's body had thrown up little the detectives did not already know and despite all the interviews, virtually no new information of any use had come to light. What seemed clear was that Marty Cundall was lying low as were Ransome and Moody. Trouble was, nobody knew where – or if they did, they were not prepared to say. Officers at all levels were becoming increasingly frustrated at the lack of progress as was the chief constable, whose phone calls to Arthur Ronald had become more frequent, more pointed and more difficult to answer.

Oddly enough, John Blizzard, the man at the very heart of the storm, was probably the least worried of all. His investigative career had been underpinned by a simple belief: that if it moved his detectives would arrest it and that if it didn't move, they would make it move then arrest it. In his experience, and he knew it smacked of superstition, such an approach brought its own luck. He had always believed that if you were trying to make things happen, you were rewarded by something unexpected – hence it was that amid all this activity, Mervyn Howatch's wife requested a meeting.

The search for Mervyn Howatch – still their prime suspect – had also drawn a frustrating blank. Uniform officers across the county were under orders to keep a look out for him, as had other forces, and officers in Western Division had been conducting intensive inquiries, carrying out door-to-door interviews, checking outhouses, searching wasteland and exploring derelict buildings. Officers from the marine unit, working with the port authority, had been scouring the riverbanks as far as the nearby sea in the hope that the body had been washed up somewhere. The Coastguard had been assisting as well, searching the seashore along the east coast a few miles from Hafton, but all to no avail; not even sweeps conducted by the force helicopter could turn anything up and the detectives were no nearer to knowing if Mervyn Howatch was alive or dead. And that meant he remained very much in the frame. Which is why the contact from his wife was so important.

After David Colley received the phone call from Janet Howatch, Blizzard left Ramsey overseeing the detectives at Abbey Road and took the sergeant to see her. As they were driving through Heston market-place on the way to Mrs

Howatch's home, the chief inspector halted the car and walked over to the gable end wall of a house. Reaching up, he cursed and tore down a poster. Crudely drawn, its message was nevertheless clear enough. It showed the Vengeance Man jabbing a finger with the message *Help me keep the neighbourhood tidy. Kill a druggie today.*

'Look at this,' said Blizzard, getting back into the car and showing the poster to his sergeant. 'He's become a bloody hero now.'

'So it would seem,' said Colley, glancing across the deserted market-place and pointing. 'They're everywhere, look.'

'We've got to get this psycho off the streets quickly,' said Blizzard grimly, slipping the car into gear. 'Otherwise they'll be electing the bastard as mayor!'

'Got to be able to do better than some of the muppets in City Hall,' replied Colley. 'So who do you think he is, guv?'

'If I knew that, I wouldn't have to go tear-arseing....'

'You know what I mean,' said Colley. 'Gut instinct?'

'I really don't know,' shrugged Blizzard as he edged the car out into the traffic. 'At the moment it comes down to two people – Mervyn Howatch or Marty Cundall – but I am not sure I can see either of them doing this kind of thing.'

'Marty's got form, though.'

'And lots of it,' nodded Blizzard, turning the car into the estate on which the Howatchs lived. 'But he hasn't got the brains to go with it. This Vengeance Man stuff? It's too imaginative for our Marty. You saw how he dealt with Eddie Barton. Marched up to him and thumped him. Marty's a meat-head. Can you really see him rooting around in his dressing-ups for a nice hat?'

'Not really,' admitted Colley.

'Besides,' and Blizzard shook his head, 'I can't help feeling that the Vengeance Man is toying with us. I mean, if he wanted to bump the lads off why go for the costume routine? It's like he's playing a game.'

'Not sure I like the rules,' said Colley sardonically as Blizzard drove them through neat roads of semi-detached houses in which were enacted routine and ordered lives, lawns mown on Saturday, cars washed and hedges clipped on Sundays, back to work on the dot of nine on Monday morning. It was the kind of life that filled the sergeant with dread, which was why he and Jay lived in a terraced house – among the real people, as Colley often said – and he did a job with irregular hours and constantly changing demands. And, for all the chief inspector lived in a modern house in a village, Colley knew Blizzard shared many of the sergeant's sentiments,

'Anyway, the reason I don't fancy Marty for this,' concluded the chief inspector, bringing the sergeant's mind back to more pressing matters and allowing himself a thin smile, 'is that he doesn't play those kind of games. He even struggles with snap.'

Colley chuckled then, as they pulled up outside a pleasant detached house in a cul-de-sac at the far end of the estate, he asked, 'So what about this guy, then?'

'Howatch is the better bet,' said Blizzard as they got out of the car and walked up the drive. 'If he has cracked up and reckons he's dying from cancer, maybe he's capable of anything. Getting even with the world before he shuffles off the mortal coil.'

'Can't see it,' said Colley with a firm shake of the head. 'Just can't see it.'

'You may be right,' said Blizzard ringing the front door bell. 'But at the moment he's the best we've got.'

The door was opened by John Pendrie.

'Fancy meeting you here,' said Blizzard acerbically. 'And fancy you remembering something else you forgot to tell us.'

'It's not like that,' said Pendrie, bridling at the tone of voice.

He led them into the living room where Janet Howatch was sitting, hunched forward, in an armchair. A small, prim little woman with mousy brown short hair and pale features, she was dressed in a patterned blue dress and a blue cardigan, which her slight frame struggled to fill. The overall impression was of someone deflated, someone gradually disappearing into herself.

'Janet,' said Colley, taking the lead because he had dealt with her before. 'This is my chief inspector, Mr Blizzard.'

She looked up at him with bloodshot eyes, which paid testament to many hours crying, and managed a weak nod.

'There is something you wanted to tell us,' said Blizzard, sitting down on the sofa and eyeing her keenly.

'I found this,' she said, holding out a crumpled piece of paper and looking at the chief inspector fearfully. 'It was in the study.'

It only had a few words on it but their importance was immense for the detectives. It was a printed agenda for a meeting of Heston Historical Society a few weeks before. The subject of the talk was John Ignatius White; the speaker was Bob Chatterton.

'Yesterday, there was an interview in the paper with Mr Chatterton,' said Janet in a voice so hoarse it was a whisper. 'He was talking about this John White person. That's when I remembered seeing that bit of paper one day. When I looked it was still there.'

Blizzard handed the piece of paper to Colley.

'How come we missed this when we searched the house?' he asked the sergeant.

'Not sure,' shrugged Colley.

'It was well concealed,' said Janet. 'Mervyn had hidden it in among some school papers in his bureau. I only found it the first time because I was dusting and accidentally knocked them on to the floor. I didn't think anything of it at the time.'

'How did your husband know about the meeting?' asked Blizzard. 'Is he a member of the historical society?'

'He is but he does not go to many of the meetings,' and

she smiled sadly. 'Too busy with school business. He's a workaholic, is my Mervyn. Always doing something.'

'But he did go to this meeting?' asked Blizzard, taking the piece of paper back from his sergeant.

'Yes.'

'How so sure?'

'I just am.'

'And what did he say afterwards about it?'

There was a long pause as Janet Howatch seemed incapable of speech. Handkerchief twisting and turning in her fingers, she sat and fought a battle within herself. The detectives let her resolve it for herself. At length she looked at them, her eyes dark and haunted.

'Do you think he killed those boys, Chief Inspector?'

Blizzard shrugged.

'I cannot say, Mrs Howatch – but perhaps what you want to tell me may help me make my mind up.'

'That's what I am afraid of.'

'You have to tell them,' interjected Pendrie, reaching out to her. 'They're bound to find out from someone. He said it to me as well – and probably others.'

She nodded, reassured as he held her hand, and looked at Blizzard, her mind made up.

'Mervyn said that perhaps John White had the right idea,' she said.

'I see,' replied Blizzard, face deadpan as he tried to conceal how the comment had indeed helped him make up his mind.

'Now what do you think, Chief Inspector?' asked Janet, looking at him in an attempt to read his thoughts.

Many had tried to read his expression before but none had ever succeeded. Not even Ronald or Colley could fathom the inner workings of Blizzard's mind sometimes. It was one of the strengths of John Blizzard in interviews that he gave nothing away, a ploy that often led suspects to assume the chief inspector knew less than he did and make the mistake of saying more than they meant to, convicting themselves from their own mouths. Blizzard was not about to give away his thoughts now but he also realized that he owed it to Janet Howatch to say something in recognition of her courage in coming forward.

'It is difficult to....' he began.

'Chief Inspector,' and there was real emotion in her voice, 'be honest with me. Please! Do you think my husband killed those boys?'

'I am being honest,' said Blizzard, and he was. 'I really do not know what to think. Just because he said it does not mean he killed them.'

'A lot of people might have said the same thing,' said Pendrie.

'Indeed,' nodded Blizzard. 'Tell me, Mrs Howatch – my sergeant here tells me that your husband was frightened of them?'

'A bit,' she nodded. 'But more angry really.'

'Angry?'

She hesitated, knowing how it must sound to the officers.

'Yes, angry,' she said at length and nodded firmly. 'He has a real temper does Mervyn. He was furious when he heard they were selling drugs. He rarely swears but he did that day.'

'Was he angry enough to harm them?'

Janet Howatch looked at him for a moment. The detectives could see the confusion in her face. At length, she said with more composure than before:

'I have only seen him lose his temper a couple of times and it was over almost as soon as it started. He was doing some DIY in the greenhouse last summer and banged his thumb with a hammer. He hurled the hammer through the greenhouse window....'

She smiled at the memory.

'Ridiculous really.'

'We've all done it,' said Blizzard, memories of injuries sustained in the engine shed coming to mind. 'And the other time?'

'A boy,' she said quietly.

'Come again?'

Suddenly the tension was back. The air was thick with it. You could almost reach out and touch it, thought Colley. He recalled Blizzard's mantra that every investigation had a turning point, a moment when everything fitted into place. You would not know it until it happened, Blizzard always said, but when it did it was like someone switching on the light. Colley wondered if this was such a moment. Blizzard's blank expression gave nothing away but they had worked together long enough for Colley to know that the chief inspector was thinking the same thing.

'Not at Heston. It happened when he was a history teacher over at Holkby Prior Comprehensive. We lived near the school. We were gardening out the front,' and she smiled again. 'He likes his gardening does Mervyn. This boy – a pupil from the school – came past. He shouted something rude about me.'

'And what did your husband do?'

'Mervyn just flipped,' and she shook her head in disbelief at the memory. 'Jumped over the wall and grabbed him by the throat. Then he punched him, knocked him to the ground.'

'What happened then?' asked Colley.

'Like I said, it was over as soon as it happened but the boy had a cut lip and his parents complained. The headteacher said that since it happened away from school, they could do nothing about. After that, Mervyn was turned down twice for promotion. He always thought that was why. That's why he went to Heston Comp. A fresh start, he said.'

She noticed the stern expressions on the detectives' faces.

'He's not a monster,' she said, 'and that was ten years ago.'

'But what about now?' asked Blizzard softly. 'You never

lose a temper, you just control it. Could he have lost control again, Mrs Howatch? Could it have led him to kill now, given the state he is in?'

'Chief Inspector,' and the voice was confused, bewildered, full of pain, 'if you had asked me before he disappeared I would have said no. I would have said I knew my husband. After twenty-one years of marriage, I could tell you what he was thinking, what he was worried about, what his dreams were. But now....'

She shrugged.

'... now it is as if I do not know him at all. I have no idea what he is thinking, what he is doing, where he is. I had no idea he was going to run away,' and she stared at them, 'how could he keep something like that from me? How could I fail to see how distressed he had become? How, Chief Inspector, how?'

Blizzard said nothing. Years of police work had taught him that there was nothing he could say when lives were falling apart and he could offer no words to this anguished woman fighting back the tears in front of him, rocking to and fro in the armchair and turning hooded eyes on him for answers he could not give. Answers only her husband could give.

'So, truthfully?' she said after regaining her composure. 'Truthfully, Chief Inspector, I have no idea if Mervyn is capable of killing those boys.'

'And what about you, Mr Pendrie?' asked Blizzard, as she lost her battle and the tears started to stream down her cheeks. 'What do you think?'

'The same,' replied Pendrie, and he looked genuinely baffled. 'You know where you are with Mervyn – know what he is going to say, what he is going to do. You can set your watch by him but this – this has changed everything.'

'Indeed it has,' murmured Blizzard, glancing down at the agenda in his hand, 'indeed it has, Mr Pendrie.'

And without further word, the detectives left the house.

Outside, Blizzard stopped on the drive and looked at his sergeant.

'Like I said,' he commented, 'he's the best we've got.'

CHAPTER **FIFTEEN**

'I know this is difficult for all you,' said Blizzard sympathetically.

Not that it sounded sympathetic. It never did. Dealing with victims was never easy for the chief inspector, who struggled with empathy. It was normally Colley, more sensitive, more warm, who brought the compassionate human touch into these situations. But although the sergeant was sitting next to him, it was Blizzard's task to open proceedings early that evening.

It was just before five thirty and it was dark outside as the two detectives sat in the dim light of a spacious lounge in one of the plush detached houses on the new estate shoehorned into a small site to the west of Heston harbour. Indeed, if Blizzard leaned over slightly he could just catch sight of the lights from the chemical plants on the far side of his beloved river, its brown waters lapping gently as they flowed irresistibly towards the sea.

Not that he had time for such prosaic thoughts now. Sitting in front of him were four people in advanced states of grief and anxiety. The house belonged to Andrea Colclough, Roger's bereaved mother, still visibly shocked at the death of her son. Her normally immaculate make-up was smudged from crying, her hair, usually perfectly groomed, looked dishevelled and uncombed, and her normally smart attire had been replaced by a grubby pullover and jeans. Aged in her late forties and a senior accountant, she was used to being in control of situations.

She made the big decisions at work and transferred that into her private life; it was she who had kicked out her husband some years before for one dalliance too many and she who had ended her four tempestuous affairs with feckless men since. The only person who had challenged her supremacy in life was her son Roger and now he was dead. This situation was something new and awful for her.

Sitting next to her on the sofa, a comforting arm around her shoulder, was Pauline Ransome, Raymond's mother, a trim bottle blonde divorcee in her early forties whose lithe body and sporty tracksuit showed her passion for the gymnasium. But, today, her usual vigour seemed to have deserted her and she eyed the detectives with understandable anxiety and, Colley thought as he watched her, more than a hint of anger. The same could be said for Tara Moody, another slim blonde divorcee, sitting on one of the armchairs. Both she and Pauline had seen what had happened to the other boys and were desperately worried for their sons. But the suppressed anger hinted at something else and the detectives waited for it to reveal itself.

Sitting conspicuously apart from the three women was Eddie Barton's mother Sandra, a cowed figure, who stared at the classic cream carpet and never raised her eyes. It was, thought Colley, sitting next to the chief inspector on one of the dining chairs, as if she was somehow ashamed of something. One thing was certain, she did not fit in with the other three. There was something different about her. She was from the other side of the tracks. She knew it and they knew it and there was definitely tension crackling in the air.

Also incongruous was the picture on the mantelpiece, next to an expensive antique clock, of a beaming, freckly gap-toothed boy of nine years old, hair neatly combed, school uniform immaculate. Roger Colclough was watching them. How times changed, thought Colley sadly. Jay had been badgering him to start a family but he kept putting it off. He told her it was not fair given the demands of his current job but in reality it was as much about fear of the unknown. Could parenthood really be this hard, he thought gazing at the cheeky face of Roger Colclough?

'And I appreciate you seeing us like this,' continued Blizzard. 'But we have reason to believe that Raymond and Paul are in serious danger. I know this is painful for you all but we need all the help we can get. I need to know where they might be hiding.'

'How would we know?' asked Pauline Ransome bitterly, 'He hasn't been in touch for nine months.'

'Same here,' nodded Tara Moody. 'Last time he was here he demanded some money and stormed off when I refused to give it to him. He smashed my car window.'

'Do you have any idea where they might be?' asked Colley. 'Anything?'

No response.

'Please, ladies,' pleaded Blizzard. 'Two boys are dead....'

Andrea Colclough started to sob, Sandra Barton continued to stare at the floor.

'And we need to find the others before someone else does,' said Blizzard, softening his tone and rebuking himself silently for his insensitivity. Not for the first time.

'I'm sorry,' said Pauline bluntly. 'Their life was a mystery to us, Chief Inspector.'

'How did they get into this?' asked Colley.

'Ask her!' said Andrea Colclough vehemently, ceasing to sob and glaring savagely at Sandra Barton. 'He led my boy astray.'

As Sandra stared with fresh intensity at the carpet, the other two women nodded their heads vigorously.

'I don't think....' began Blizzard

'He corrupted our boys,' said Pauline Ransome. 'Before they met him, they were nice boys. He came to tea once – did nothing but swear.'

'Hardly a crime,' murmured Blizzard beneath his breath.

'If my boy had stayed with people from this side of town instead of his type....' spat Pauline.

'This is hardly the time for this discussion,' said Blizzard firmly.

'What type?' asked Sandra Barton suddenly, lifting her head and staring defiantly at the others.

'Your type don't belong,' said Tara Moody, and she looked at the detectives and added, 'she's a cleaner, you know.'

As if that explained everything. Which it did – if only about Tara and her 'type'.

'I'm not sure that makes any difference,' said Blizzard.

'Eddie Barton was a low-life,' said Tara nastily. 'Our boys had never been in trouble before they met him. Then what happens? Suddenly they're getting themselves into all sorts of aggravation with the school.'

'Listen,' said Blizzard, sensing this was not the time to suggest that they were already into bullying before hooking up with Eddie Barton, 'whatever issues you women have between yourselves are none of our concern. I need to know where to find Raymond and Paul before the killer does and that's all I care about. I ask again, do you have any idea where they might have been hiding out after the last robbery?'

'You have no evidence my boy was involved in those robberies,' protested Tara Moody as Pauline Ransome nodded in agreement. 'Besides, it was probably Eddie who....'

'Come on, sergeant,' said Blizzard wearily, standing up and heading for the door, watched by the surprised women. 'We are getting nowhere here.'

'I'll come with you,' said Sandra Barton quickly, pulling on her coat and walking down the hallway with them.

Once the front door had shut behind them, Blizzard halted in the driveway.

'Would you care to explain what that was all about, Mrs Barton?'

'They never accepted me,' she said sadly. 'It was the same with all the incomers.'

'Incomers?'

'Heston Comprehensive splits into two. People like them,' and she nodded at the house, 'and people like me. They think they own the world and they resent people like us coming into "their" area and sending our children to "their" school. They're always making snide comments. It's like a scab they have to keep picking at. They never accepted me and never will. Goodnight, Chief Inspector.'

And she walked down the drive towards her Mini Metro car.

'Suddenly,' said Blizzard. 'I have become very cynical about life.'

'Become?' asked Colley.

CHAPTER **SIXTEEN**

'What all this shows,' mused John Blizzard, lifting the glass of red wine to the light and eyeing it appreciatively as he swilled it gently in the light of the table map, 'lovely drop, Jay, bit classy for David, mind – is how lives reach out to touch each other in ways we can never know.'

'Very philosophical,' said Jay with a twinkle in her eye. 'For a Plod.'

It was that evening and after the detectives had worked late checking out elements of Janet Howatch's story, Colley had invited Blizzard back to the house he shared with Jay for dinner. After nipping home for a shower and changing into a casual shirt and dark slacks, Blizzard arrived with a bottle of best Italian red shortly after eight and, walking into the narrow hallway, sniffed the air appreciatively as the smell of cooking pasta wafted towards him. He walked into the kitchen, gave Jay, a willowy redhead, an affectionate peck on the cheek and peered with approval into the bubbling pan on the hob. As a divorced man who lived alone, Blizzard sometimes missed the comfortable domestic life and always enjoyed his visit to Colley's home, not least because Jay knew he loved Italian food. After eating, the three of them settled down in the tastefully decorated living room with its pastel shades and rustic prints and soft light afforded by a couple of table lamps and the flickering fake coal fire.

Blizzard was in an armchair, glass of wine in hand,

Colley was in another with his usual can of bitter, not a man of cosmopolitan tastes David Colley, and Jay was curled up on the sofa with her own glass of wine. The comment about interlocking lives from John Blizzard broke the rules of their get-togethers, which had always been easy, relaxed affairs, partly because they banned shop talk. But, mellowed by his third glass of wine – Jay had opened another bottle – Blizzard had started to talk about the events of recent weeks.

'What do you mean?' asked Jay.

'I shouldn't,' said Blizzard with a shake of the head. 'Shop talk.'

'I'm interested. View it as a discussion about sociology rather than police work.'

'Well,' said Blizzard contemplatively. 'Look at those four lads. They have touched so many lives. There's Mervyn Howatch driven to god knows what by them, his wife with her life blown apart because of the stress on her husband, the boys' mothers consumed with grief and guilt and anger and who knows what, those parents who packed the school hall all furious that their children were being offered drugs, Marty Cundall driven to violence....'

'Like he needed much driving,' grunted Colley.

'Nevertheless,' nodded Blizzard, 'it was Barton and his drug selling that brought it about.'

'You sound like Pauline Ransome,' said Colley quickly. 'They were all at it, remember.'

'Thank you for the reminder,' said Blizzard, mildly annoyed at his slip. 'What I am saying is that everywhere you look, there are people touched by these lives. Dozens of them. Hundreds of them maybe.'

'And your point is?' asked Jay.

'I'm not sure,' confessed Blizzard. 'I suppose one of the points is that so many people knew what those kids were like yet they all let them get away with it. Preferred to stay silent or engage in feuds like we witnessed this evening with the mothers. Someone should have nipped this in the bud. The school – look at the school – it knew what was happening.'

'So do you blame the teachers?' asked Jay keenly.

Blizzard, mindful that she taught in a primary school, shook his head quickly.

'Not entirely.'

'But to some extent?'

'Only to the extent that we are all to blame,' said Blizzard, warming to his theme, 'Did the school crack down on them hard enough? Did the police do enough? Did the parents do enough? Did I do enough?'

'What about self-determination?' asked Jay. 'Surely, there is a danger in blaming everyone but the kids themselves?'

'You sound like John Pendrie,' said Blizzard acerbically.

She laughed.

'You know him?' asked Blizzard.

'Oh, yes, what you might call a liberal. If you want to look at someone who failed in their job, look at him,' and she clapped a hand to her mouth. 'Shouldn't have said that. You were right about not talking shop, John.'

'You've said it now. What did you mean?'

'A friend of mine knows him. She used to teach at Heston Comp. She says he is weak, doesn't like anything that smacks of getting tough with the pupils. He says the kids have to make their own minds up about things. Trouble is, the kids have him marked down as a bit of a softie.'

'I'll bet they do,' said Colley, taking a gulp of his beer, 'no wonder Barton and his mates thought they could get away with it.'

'I'll bet he and Mervyn Howatch have some right old arguments,' said Blizzard.

'They do,' and Jay lowered her voice, in that irrational way that people do when they confess things in the privacy of their own home. 'This didn't come from me but I heard that the governors appointed Pendrie as deputy headteacher against Mervyn Howatch's wishes. Mervyn likes to present this image as a tough headmaster and that's not John Pendrie's style at all but he came over brilliantly at interview. Ticked all the boxes. It was never going to work.'

'Indeed,' said Blizzard, and gave her a mischievous look. 'And where, Miss Priest, do you stand?'

'Me,' she said with a butter-wouldn't-melt expression, 'I just lock them in the caretaker's shed if they play up. Works wonders after a week or two. Obviously, they've gone blind and have lost the capacity for independent movement but you can't have everything.'

Blizzard roared with laughter. That was one of the reasons he loved visiting their house because it helped banish, if only for an hour or two, the tough world in which he and Dave Colley were forced to work.

CHAPTER **SEVENTEEN**

B ob Chatterton's welcoming smile faded when he saw the grim expressions on the detectives' faces as, shortly after four the next afternoon, they stood on his doorstep. The detectives had gone to the historian's house, a former fisherman's cottage close to the harbour in Heston, after a Monday morning spent checking out more elements of Janet Howatch's story and an afternoon assessing what they had learnt. Now they felt ready to confront Bob Chatterton. There were questions they needed answering.

'Is something wrong?' he asked, standing uneasily on the doorstep.

'I think that might depend on what you tell us,' said Blizzard.

Chatterton led them into his cramped little living room, on the walls of which hung several sepia prints depicting scenes from the village's fishing past, and an old lobster pot, battered and encrusted with sea salt. There were a couple of antique bookcases crammed with history books, most of them about the sea.

'My father was a fisherman,' he explained, relaxing slightly and noticing Blizzard's interest. 'The lobster pot was his. So were most of the books. I think you know these two gentlemen?'

Blizzard nodded and extended a hand to Chatterton's guests. Albert Prendergast was sitting at a table by the window at the far end of the cluttered little room, papers spread out in front of him. His son David was in an armchair, newspaper spread out on his lap. The detectives were not surprised to see him; they had seen the white pick-up bearing his name parked outside.

'A delight again, gentlemen,' said the chief inspector. 'I hope I am not interrupting anything.'

'Nothing that can't wait,' said Albert. 'Myself and Bob are only planning the next programme for the historical society.'

'I take it you are not a member?' said Blizzard, gesturing to David's newspaper.

'Not my scene really, Chief Inspector. But my dad needed a lift. Besides I like to encourage him,' and he smiled gently. 'Keeps him off the streets and out of trouble. We don't want any more unfortunate incidents, do we, dad?'

Albert smiled fondly at the jest.

'Please sit down, gentlemen,' said Chatterton, gesturing to a threadbare sofa. 'I know it is not particularly salubrious but it was my father's and I cannot bring myself to throw it out. I like to think it has character.'

'Among other things,' said Blizzard dubiously as he sat down and noticed a couple of brown stains on the arm.

'I like it,' said Colley, preferring it to the sterile surroundings of most of the houses in Heston he had visited over the past few days.

'Somehow I do not think Jay would agree,' murmured the chief inspector, thinking of the cool and classy living room the sergeant's girlfriend had fashioned at the couple's home and in which they had drunk far more than was good for them the previous evening. Blizzard had been popping the aspirin all morning.

'Maybe,' grinned Colley, adding wistfully. 'Nevertheless....'

'So what can I do for you?' asked Chatterton, sitting down on a battered armchair. 'I assume it is about what happened to those boys?'

'It is,' nodded Blizzard. 'I want to know about Mervyn Howatch.'

'Mervyn?' asked Chatterton. 'Why?'

'Who is he?' asked Albert Prendergast.

'The headteacher at Heston Comp,' said his son. 'Nice man. Came to the house once.'

'Oh, yes, I remember,' nodded Albert. 'Very earnest chap as I recall. Sticky-up hair.'

'That's him,' said Blizzard.

'Didn't seem to do much smiling.'

'That's him,' said his son.

The two of them chuckled.

'How do you know him?' asked the chief inspector.

'I play quoits over at Aniston,' said David. 'Mervyn Howatch is a member. Very good player, in fact. Won the club championship last year. But why do you want to know about him?'

'I think I am right in saying that he came to your talk on John White, Bob?' said Blizzard to Chatterton.

'Yes, he did,' nodded Chatterton. 'Back in September I think it was. But why do you want to know? I assume it is something to do with his disappearance?'

'Partly.'

'Surely,' said David Prendergast slowly, realization dawning, 'you cannot be suggesting that Mervyn Howatch is responsible for killing those boys, Chief Inspector?'

'I am not suggesting anything,' said Blizzard coolly.

He had learned long ago that giving nothing away was the best policy unless it served his purposes. No comeback that way – but he didn't mind people guessing and he could see the three men considering the implications of his question now. He also noticed that the friendly smiles had became a little more guarded.

'Did he appear interested in your talk?' asked Colley, taking over the questioning from his colleague.

'Yes, he did,' said Chatterton, adding quickly. 'But it was an academic interest, Sergeant. Mervyn's background was as a history teacher. He was interested in that kind of thing. And surely you cannot think that....'

'We are just checking some things out,' said Blizzard, 'Did he ever talk about John White after your talk?'

'Well, as a matter of fact he approached me a week or so later and asked some more questions.'

'And why would he do that?' asked Blizzard.

'We shared an interest in history,' said Chatterton. 'You should appreciate our passion, Chief Inspector. Indeed, it was Mervyn who asked me to teach at the school.'

'You taught at Heston Comp?' asked Blizzard, surprised.

'Yes. Just for a term. I was a supply teacher. Taught history. Their usual teacher was off with a back problem.'

'When was this?'

'Five-six years ago, I forget the actual dates.'

'Were Eddie Barton and his mates there at the time?' asked Colley.

'Yes, they were,' nodded Chatterton. 'But I did not really get involved with them ...: thank goodness. I know you should not speak ill of the dead but they were a nasty lot, Sergeant.'

'So,' said Blizzard, not wishing to seem too interested in the new revelation – he had already decided he was going to ask Colley to go back and dig around a little more into Chatterton's time at the school – 'getting back to Mervyn, did he express an unnatural interest in your story about John White?'

'Might I say,' interjected David Prendergast, a slight edge in his voice, 'that although I can see the reason for your questions, Mr Blizzard, Mervyn Howatch is a decent human being and I can't see him turning to murder. I mean, can you?'

And he looked intently at the chief inspector.

'Like I said, I am not sure what to think,' replied Blizzard, choosing his words carefully. 'But whoever carried out these murders knew about John White.'

'Granted,' nodded David. 'But it's a big leap of reasoning.'

'Indeed,' acknowledged Blizzard. 'Nevertheless, the

killer has to be someone who knew about the story – and, sadly, that means we have to check out people who were at the meeting. That is why we asked for that list of everyone present, Bob – although as I recall, Mervyn Howatch's name was not on it?'

'To be honest, Chief Inspector, I did not check the list,' said Chatterton. 'It was signed by everyone present and put in our file. I simply let you have a copy. Nothing sinister. It's not a cover-up.'

'I am sure it isn't. So why wasn't his name on it?'

'As I recall, Mervyn arrived late – he had been detained at school over something. I imagine the attendance list had been circulated and returned before he arrived.'

'OK,' nodded Blizzard.

It seemed reasonable.

'But he did seem interested in the story of John White?' said Colley.

'Indeed he did, Sergeant,' said Chatterton, adding earnestly, 'but I repeat, Mervyn's interest was as a historian. It was purely academic. He had a particular fascination in the era of Cromwell's Protectorate. As I recall, his university thesis was about Cromwell and his interest stemmed from that. He said that when he retired he would write a book about that period of history. That was the only reason he was so interested.'

'You may be right,' nodded Blizzard, standing up, 'but I have to ask.'

'We appreciate that,' said David Prendergast and he smiled, 'but in this country, loving history is not yet a crime, is it? My father would be under arrest if it was – as would you, Chief Inspector.'

Blizzard allowed himself a wry grin.

'No,' he said, extending a hand, 'no it isn't a crime, although when you hear philistines like our sergeant here talk about my passion for railways, you could be forgiven for thinking it was. Thank you for your help, gentlemen.'

The detectives left the cottage and walked back to the car in silence.

'What you thinking?' asked Colley.

'I am thinking three things,' said Blizzard, glancing at his watch. 'The first and by far the most important is that the nice pub in the market-place will be open – fancy a pint before we knock off for the day?'

'Is the Pope a Catholic?'

'Never been religious but I'll take that as a yes.'

'And the second thing?'

'That it all sounded very plausible and that I am increasingly unsure about Mervyn Howatch as our killer.'

'And the third?'

'That I want to find out more about Bob Chatterton's time at Heston Comp. Even if it was only for a term, it might cast some light on things. History may not be a crime … but murder certainly is.'

'I'll get on to it,' nodded the sergeant.

'Thanks,' said Blizzard, unlocking the car door. 'And keep it low key. No need for him to know about it at this stage but, like I always say….'

'When you shake a tree there's no telling what will fall out,' continued the sergeant, having heard it a thousand times before.

'That's my boy,' said Blizzard. 'There's hope for you yet.'

They were about to get into the car when the door of the cottage opened and Bob Chatterton ran down the street towards them.

'Chief Inspector,' he said breathlessly. 'We have been talking – and there is something you should know.'

'Shaking trees,' beamed Blizzard.

CHAPTER **EIGHTEEN**

Squalls of rain swept along the river, blown in from the North Sea by a wind that had also brought the grey clouds to which the residents of Hafton were so accustomed. It was a fact, according to weather records, that Hafton had more rain than any other English city except Manchester and now it was falling heavily as dusk settled over the river. On the far side, the chemical plant lights twinkled and Blizzard could see the flash of car headlamps on the road snaking its way along the bank. Blizzard had been standing there for half an hour, just staring, oblivious to the rain as he contemplated what he was about to do.

Bob Chatterton's revelation an hour or so before had cast new light on the situation in a way that was as spectacular as it was unexpected as it was confusing. The afternoon's events had born out yet again Blizzard's theory that if you put some effort in, as the detectives had with their aggressive pursuing of new leads throughout the day, reward would come from unexpected sources.

Which was where Bob Chatterton, and the revelations he had laid out before them when they went back into his cottage, came into things. Having kept his secret for several months, he had found the mounting pressure intolerable, particularly given the events of the past fortnight. Despite being frightened of betraying the man who had taken him into his confidence – it was part-principle and part-fear of crossing such a strong individual that had held him back – Chatterton had finally resolved to seek advice. A problem shared is a problem halved so in a hurried conversation with the Prendergasts after the detectives left the cottage, Bob Chatterton had been persuaded to tell what he knew.

Intrigued, Blizzard and Colley had listened to his story, as dusk fell and the winter gloom deepened in the cottage, and had then headed back to Abbey Road Police Station. After briefing a disbelieving Arthur Ronald, who at one point buried his head in his hands, Blizzard had bid Colley good night – the sergeant was due to go to the cinema with Jay – and had intended to head for home for a glass or two of whisky, a good book and an early night to recharge batteries which the pressures of such a high profile investigation had largely drained. But after leaving the police station, Blizzard had found himself, as so often in the past, drawn to his favourite spot on the foreshore of the River Haft, the same spot where Mervyn Howatch's car had been abandoned. The irony was not lost on the chief inspector.

He often came here to think, to escape the bustle of the city, and to stand staring out over the industrial river that he had grown to love. As a man who grew up in the countryside, it always amazed him that he should have developed such an affinity for a river like the Haft with its murky waters, chemical tankers and rust-bucket dredgers. Part of an affinity with industrial history fashioned through his passion for steam locomotives, he assumed. And the Haft had plenty of industrial history. The lifeblood of the city for centuries, the Haft had become one of the most important industrial rivers in the north in the nineteenth and early twentieth centuries, its jetties and harbours providing safe haven for the ships that plied the seven seas in pursuit of trade and exploration. Today the ships had all but gone except for the chemical tankers.

During the 1800s, there had been the factories as well; huge affairs that sprung up along the north side of the river, engineering plants, shipyards, armaments factories, as well as large warehouses operated by the city's fruit importers. Much of that had also gone now and Hafton was in what the politicians called a state of regeneration with derelict riverside sites being brought back to life as gleaming business parks, all glass and fancy sculptures. They did not have the same character, Blizzard always thought; indeed, he had much preferred the sense of dereliction that had symbolized the riverbank for so many years. There was something beguiling, something real about it. It gave the city a sense of identity. Sterile glass-fronted office blocks with fancy logos did not. Despite his acceptance that regeneration was needed, he could not help feeling that those areas of industrial decay, with their derelict factories, ramshackle outbuildings, piles of wire and scrap metal and disused railway lines were the real Hafton. It was not a popular view at a time when millions were being ploughed into creating a new-look city but one the chief inspector held to it all the same.

Yet despite all the changes, the river retained its character and something about the Haft brought Blizzard back time and time again to stare over its dark waters and think. Like the engine shed housing the Old Lady, it was something to do with the sense of peace he could find here, the sense of being in the middle of thousands of people yet still being alone. It was a feeling he liked and it allowed him to think clearly in a way not possible amid the telephone calls and constant to-ing and fro-ing that formed the heart of any major inquiry.

And this time there was much to think about. As Blizzard stood, collar turned up against the rain, he mulled over the events of the day and in particular, Bob Chatterton's information. They were words that had directed him inevitably to a single plan of action but nevertheless, Ronald's final words, uttered as the chief inspector had left his friend's office less than a hour ago, came back to him, almost as if they floated across the choppy waters of the Haft.

'You had better play this right,' Ronald had said. 'Get it wrong and we can all start writing out parking tickets.'

It was a warning – one that Ronald often repeated when the chief inspector was outlining a potentially controversial line of inquiry – and one to which Blizzard now gave great attention as he stood staring out over the river and formulating his plan for the following morning.

CHAPTER **NINETEEN**

Next morning a thick winter fog, damp and dank, rolled in off the river and shrouded Hafton as the small police convoy headed through the deserted streets and out to the very western edge of the city. After a few minutes they had entered another world, where the stinking blocks of flats and glass-strewn council estates seemed almost like a distant memory. Even the trim and proper housing estates of places like Heston seemed to recede into the distance as Blizzard's car and two marked patrol vehicles drove steadily into the most opulent part of Hafton. This was where the money lived and the detectives rarely had need to visit it, unless it was to investigate a burglary. Riding with Blizzard, Colley could only recall having ever been to the area three times in his years at Western. The reason was that virtually all the owners had hi-tech security systems, surveillance cameras, sophisticated alarms and, like the house they had come to visit, a high perimeter wall. Only the most determined and very best of burglars would try screwing a house here.

For all that, such security was needed because these house owners were worth millions and many had invested some of that money on valuable paintings and antique ornaments. The occupant of the house they were approaching was typical, a man who had made a small fortune through myriad business activities and whose private life was as impenetrable as his public life was accessible for all to see. As such, his house was protected not only by a high red brick wall but by ornate wrought iron gates through which they could glimpse a large ivy-covered mock Georgian mansion set in its own landscaped grounds and approached via a winding gravel drive lined with classical statues.

'I'm in the wrong job,' grunted Blizzard, peering through at the two Bentleys parked in the drive as he pressed the buzzer at the gate.

'Police,' he said when a voice answered.

The gates slowly swung open and, leaving the uniforms out on the road, the detectives walked slowly up the drive, feet crunching on the gravel.

'Are you sure about this?' asked Colley, as they approached the house.

'No.'

'Now you tell me.'

'But just because these people have got lots of money doesn't mean they're above the law.'

'But this fellow?' protested Colley. 'I can't see it.'

'To be honest, neither can I,' admitted Blizzard. 'But we have to ask. Who knows, maybe something will come of it. God knows, we need a breakthrough. Even Ronald is starting to ask questions.'

The front door was open when they arrived and standing at the top of the steps was the man they had come to see. Even though it was just before seven, he was dressed immaculately in a black suit with a classy pale blue silk tie. He did not seem surprised that they were there. Nor did he seemed unduly concerned.

'Good morning, Chief Inspector,' he said calmly. 'So who has been blabbing then – as if I didn't know?'

'Good morning, Mr Stanshall,' said Blizzard, gesturing down the drive to the waiting police car. 'Shall we?'

'It is really necessary?'

'I'd rather talk down the station.'

Stanshall shrugged and less than an hour later they were sitting in an interview room at Abbey Road, Blizzard and

Colley on one side and Stanshall and his lawyer on the other. Blizzard had not had dealings with the solicitor before, not surprising since his was a high class law firm in Hafton and his clients moved in spheres way above the world inhabited by the people Blizzard and his team tended to question. Indeed, Philip D'eath looked slightly uncomfortable to be there. Aged in his late fifties, he was an elegant man, his brown hair immaculately combed – got to be a weave, Colley reflected idly as he waited for proceedings to begin – and dressed in a black hand-made pinstripe suit complete with red handkerchief, poking out of the breast pocket.

The lawyer's discomfort was caused because he normally dealt with clients' business problems and was much more at home in the world of City finance and top drawer business deals than in the stuffy, sparse interview room of a police station. If the truth be told, he had only ever been in one police interview room before, years ago when one of his clients was arrested for embezzlement. It had not been a particularly successful experience; the businessman had gone to jail for two years. D'eath had always feared a knock on the door from the police because, under duress from his client, and admittedly, the offer of a huge fee, he had ensured that his client was able to spirit away much of his ill-gotten gains in offshore bank accounts. Colley noticed that the lawyer was sweating and smiled: he and Blizzard liked it when lawyers perspired. Like pigs at the trough, the chief inspector often said with a gleam in his eye. Showed they were uneasy and robbed them of a little bit of dignity. Handed the initiative to the police, he said.

'Is my client under arrest?' asked D'eath, aware that his palms were clammy.

'No, he is not,' replied Blizzard coolly. 'He is free to walk out of this room at any time.'

'Then perhaps we should....'

'But if he does walk out,' continued Blizzard, an edge in

his voice. 'It will leave some important questions unanswered. There may be a perfectly legitimate explanation for all of this – and I am sure your client would like the opportunity to furnish me with it.'

'It's OK, Philip,' said Stanshall, flapping a hand at his lawyer. 'I want this cleared up.'

'I am sure we can agree on that,' nodded Blizzard.

'So what do you want to know?' asked Stanshall. 'And since I can guess why I am here, can I ask who told you?'

'I can't answer that,' replied Blizzard. 'You know that, Mr Stanshall.'

'Bob Chatterton, I imagine,' said Stanshall dismissively. 'I said he wouldn't be able to keep his trap shut, didn't I, Philip?'

The lawyer said nothing. Neither did Blizzard but he was acutely aware that Bob Chatterton and the Prendergasts had given him the information about Stanshall in order to deflect attention away from Mervyn Howatch, a man Blizzard liked much more as a suspect than the brash, pushy businessman. Although in one light, the information could be seen as potentially incriminating, Blizzard also had a strong sense that Stanshall had been offered up to get Howatch off the hook. It was, in short, a set-up.

But, as far as the chief inspector was concerned, and doubts notwithstanding, Robert Stanshall was still very much wriggling on the end of that hook. For a moment, and not for the first time, the thought transported him back to a childhood spent fishing with his father on the streams and becks of rural Lincolnshire. Sometimes, thought Blizzard, he wished he could roll back time and be seven years old again. But he couldn't and there was work to do. For the moment, Robert Stanshall had some questions to answer.

'Anyway, you don't need to tell me it was Chatterton,' continued Stanshall. 'I know it's the little weasel.'

'Let me tell you what we know,' said Blizzard. 'A day or

two after Bob Chatterton's talk in September, you went round to see him and started asking lots of questions about John Ingatius White. Is that true?'

'Yes.'

'Tell me why.'

Stanshall turned to his lawyer and said calmly, 'Philip, if you will.'

The lawyer opened his briefcase and produced a document.

'If anything,' said the solicitor, handing it to his client, 'my client is guilty of bad taste rather than anything criminal.'

'Not exactly the kind of unqualified support I would have liked,' murmured Stanshall, glancing sharply at his lawyer.

'You know my feelings on this, Robert,' replied D'eath archly. 'I warned you about this right from the start.'

The solicitor turned to the chief inspector.

'I ought to say that all of this is very much against my advice.'

'Whatever,' said Blizzard.

'Nevertheless, you can't charge anyone with bad taste,' said D'eath.

'Unfortunately not,' murmured Blizzard, 'otherwise that half-wit that designed that sculpture in front of City Hall would be slopping out by now.'

Colley smiled and after a moment or two's hesitation, so did Stanshall and his lawyer. The comment had eased the tension somewhat, testament perhaps to Blizzard's belief that Stanshall was not his man.

'This document,' said Stanshall, pushing it across the table to the detectives, 'is from the design firm I use at the theme park.'

Blizzard looked at it and raised an eyebrow.

'A fairground attraction?' he asked.

'I prefer the phrase themed attraction,' said Stanshall, a tone of effrontery in his voice. 'Fairground gives the wrong connotation. Besides, this is not some coconut shy, Chief Inspector. It would cost a couple of million pounds. I got the idea when I heard Bob give his talk. We are always looking out for new rides and this seemed tailor-made.'

'How would it work?' asked Colley, glancing at the paper, fascinated by the drawings spread out in front of them.

'It would be designed as a big graveyard,' said Stanshall, eyes gleaming as he outlined the plan. 'You would go in one end and have to pick your way through the cemetery in the dark. There would be lots of screams and other scary noises. And lots of swirling fog. As you worked your way through, John White would leap out at you at various points. It would have been absolutely terrific.'

Colley, who had loved fairgrounds when he was a child, nodded, eyes bright.

'It would,' he said enthusiastically, forgetting where he was for a moment. 'The fog's a master stroke!'

Blizzard raised an eyebrow – fairgrounds had never been his thing. Colley mouthed 'sorry'.

'And I know what you are thinking,' said Stanshall calmly. 'Did he invent the Vengeance Man and carry out those killings to ensure there was lots of publicity when the ride opens in the summer?'

'The thought had occurred,' murmured Blizzard, declining to add that it had occurred for only a moment and that Stanshall was only here to eliminate himself from the investigation.

Blizzard had said the same thing to Ronald the night before and the superintendent had only reluctantly agreed to the interview even though he was still concerned that Stanshall could make a lot of trouble, go to the media, sue for wrongful arrest, complain to the chief constable, of whose Lodge Ronald knew the businessman was a member. But the police officer in him realized that it was an interview that had to take place.

'Not surprising that you thought that way,' said

Stanshall. 'Although in fact, the murders have probably wrecked the plan.'

'Why?'

'I can't do it now,' said Stanshall with a sad shake of the head. 'What with those two boys dead.'

His lawyer looked at him in surprise.

'That's a change in tune,' he said.

'I know,' said Stanshall. 'I've already invested £100,000 in this idea – design firms do like to rip people off, perhaps you would like to investigate them one day, Chief Inspector. At first I thought it might still be a goer despite what had happened, perhaps when all the hoo-ha died down. But whenever I did it, it would cause all sorts of problems. I know they say all publicity is good publicity but can you imagine the furore, Chief Inspector? Those bereaved mums slagging me off in the media? I'd be crucified. Not a good strategy at all, particularly when I have just started to win over some of the blue rinse brigade who opposed the opening of the theme park.'

'I can see your point,' said Blizzard, adding acerbically, 'but what other people think has not usually prevented you from doing something. You rode roughshod over public opinion when you applied for permission to build your theme park.'

'Point taken,' nodded Stanshall, 'but hacking off a few hoity-toity old fogies in the villages is a different thing from being seen to take advantage of dead boys. I admit that for some people, it might actually make the ride more attractive but on balance it's not good PR. So I have decided to shelve it. Those lads might have been scumbags but I can't be seen to be taking advantage of their deaths. Bad for business. Ironic really.'

'Ironic?'

'Well, the Vengeance Man himself has killed the idea stone dead,' and Stanshall gave a crooked smile.

'How much did Bob Chatterton know about your plans?' asked Colley.

'Not all the details but he knew the general idea. I asked him to keep quiet about it,' said Stanshall. 'You need to keep the lid on these things. Very competitive world, theme parks. Didn't want someone half-inching the idea and doing it first. Old Robbie over at World of Wonder at Bruton would just love that.'

'And how, pray, did you keep Chatterton quiet?' asked Blizzard.

'I said I might pay for his nasty little book to be published but I guess he got cold feet,' and he smiled again. 'Unfortunately, Chief Inspector, the idea is dead in the water – rather like good old John Ignatius White.'

Blizzard sighed. It might not have been the best of phrases to use but he couldn't have put it better himself.

'Can my client go now?' asked D'eath, struggling to retain some dignity.

Blizzard wafted wearily at the door.

'Go on. David, see these good gentlemen off the premises, please.'

'Before we go,' said the lawyer, irritated that he had been turfed out of bed so early and embarrassed at the cursory way his client had treated him, 'can I just say that I have a good mind to complain to....'

'Can it,' said Stanshall in that blunt way of his when dealing with those for whom he had little respect, 'I have no desire to take this any further. I stood up at the public meeting and demanded that the police do something – well they have. They brought me in for questioning.'

'Yes,' protested D'eath, 'but....'

'Besides,' said Stansall, cutting across him, 'I'd have brought me in as well. You have to admit it makes me a pretty decent suspect.'

And, getting to his feet, he winked mischievously at the detectives.

'Good day to you, Chief Inspector,' he said before disappearing into the corridor, his solicitor trailing behind like a small child that had been scolded by its parent.

Blizzard watched them go and sighed. When Colley re-entered the room a few moments later, the chief inspector eyed him quizzically.

'The fog's a master stroke?' he repeated, giving his sergeant a pained look. 'What kind of talk is that?'

Colley grinned.

CHAPTER **TWENTY**

I t was just before five on the following Monday afternoon that Derek Stoddart was shot. After a few days of
frustratingly fruitless inquiries, it was the last thing John
Blizzard needed. A view with which Derek Stoddart would
presumably have agreed, had he been capable of speech
after the murderous assault. The shop owner did not have
a chance. Two men walked into his shop in Heston, armed
with sawn-off shotguns, and instructed him to empty his
till at gunpoint, watched in horror by a teenage shop assistant and a middle-aged woman customer.

Stoddart handed over the money but as they turned to
leave, the store owner made as if to grab them and one of
the robbers coolly pointed his gun and blasted him in the
chest. Stoddart was hurled backwards, bringing a shelf of
cigarettes crashing down on top of him. As he fell to the
floor, clutching his chest from which blood spurted in a
wide scarlet arc, the men turned and walked calmly from
the shop. Seconds later, the witnesses heard a car engine
roar into life and the robbers had disappeared. Their car –
stolen earlier that day – was later found abandoned on
wasteland over on the eastern side of the city but the men
were long gone.

Now, John Blizzard stood in the mini-mart and gazed
down at the ugly bloodstain on the floor behind the counter
and the mess of cigarette packets. Moments earlier, he had
checked with the hospital, the one where the other shopkeeper was recovering, if slowly, after being shot and was
told that Derek Stoddart was undergoing emergency surgery.

'Deliberate,' Blizzard said grimly as he and Colley watched the forensics team get to work. 'They didn't need to shoot him. This was an execution.'

'Unless they panicked,' said Colley, 'one of the witnesses said he grabbed at them.'

'Maybe,' nodded Blizzard, 'but one thing is sure, it's got to be Ransome and Moody.'

'There were just two of them,' nodded Colley.

'It's not just that. The level of violence as well. How many shop robberies have we had in the division in the past decade, David?'

'Dunno,' shrugged the sergeant. 'Forty-fifty, maybe?'

'And how many times have the guns actually been used?'

'Take the point,' nodded Colley. 'Two. The one where that guy was shot in the leg and this one.'

'Got to be them – and they're getting more desperate,' said Blizzard and glanced at the smartly dressed officer walking across the shop to them.

'Bit grubby for you, isn't it?' asked Blizzard sardonically.

Detective Inspector Graham Ross, head of forensics, allowed himself a grin. If he had a penny for every time he had heard that joke from the chief inspector, he would be a rich man. Immaculate as ever in pressed grey suit with red silk tie, black shoes shining, and with his brown wavy hair beautifully groomed as usual, he was accustomed to the sartorially-challenged chief inspector's friendly jibes. The banter between them was one of the things he liked about working with Blizzard. The other was that the chief inspector was straight in his dealings. None of those subtle hints that all was not well; if Blizzard was unhappy he said it. And even though that could sometimes make life uncomfortable, Ross preferred it that way.

'Yeah,' he said straight-faced. 'Rather be in a Versace emporium than here but there you are, can't have everything.'

Colley chuckled.

'Anything?' asked Blizzard.

'Well,' said Ross, 'it definitely looks like the others. I'll have to see what ballistics say but it sounds like the same weapon.'

'Prints?'

'Gloves, I am afraid.'

'Dammit,' exclaimed Blizzard, 'there must be something.'

'We've not got much to work with really.'

'OK,' nodded Blizzard and Ross went back to work.

'Bang goes your theory that they would lie low,' said Colley. 'But why keep robbing? They know every police officer in the city is after them. There must be a reason to risk breaking cover.'

'Indeed there must. Listen, that informant who said Barton's boys were the robbers – can we go back to him and see if he knows any more?'

'I'll try,' said Colley doubtfully, 'but he has gone to ground.'

'Try anyway,' said Blizzard, as they headed out into the street, 'they obviously need the money badly, otherwise they wouldn't be taking so many risks. I want to know why and I want to know why they targeted Derek Stoddart as well.'

'His shops do well.'

'Yeah, they do but there's more to it than that, I'm sure of it. Why leave the message here?'

'He's been pretty outspoken in the media,' said Colley.

'Crims don't take any notice of that,' said Blizzard, unlocking the door to his car. 'No, there's something more to it. I want to find out everything we can about Derek Stoddart.'

'Maybe they heard that he had been talking to Marty Cundall about protection.'

'Maybe,' said Blizzard. 'Whatever it was, they came after him deliberately.'

The radio crackled.

'Message for Chief Inspector Blizzard,' said a disembodied voice. 'Hospital says Derek Stoddart is now out of surgery but the doctors say he has only a ten per cent chance of survival.'

'And now,' said Blizzard grimly, 'they've got him....'

CHAPTER **TWENTY-ONE**

lizzard always said that what you did not know was more important than what you did, a truism that was about to be proved yet again as one of their lines of inquiry bore spectacular fruit. It was late Wednesday afternoon two days after Derek Stoddart had been shot and the team of detectives had been involved in frenetic inquiries, conducted against the backdrop of the shop owner's desperate fight for survival on a life support machine at the local hospital. Blizzard had gone to see him the previous evening and had stood for some minutes, grimly surveying the ashen face and the array of tubes and wires keeping him alive.

The shooting had a serious effect on Heston with patrol officers reporting a palpable sense of fear among residents and shopkeepers complaining that business had plummeted and that it had become impossible to persuade staff to work. At least one shop had closed down. Against that backdrop, Blizzard desperately needed a breakthrough and he needed it quickly. When it came, it came from outside Hafton, in a call shortly before lunchtime, from David Colley, sitting in his car on a roadside in Cumbria and talking rapidly into his telephone.

Two hours later, as Blizzard sat digesting what he had been told, he was suddenly forced, much against his will, to negotiate a tricky situation better suited to Ronald's diplomatic skills than his own less tolerant approach to life. It came, as so often over recent weeks, in the form of Chris

Ramsey who had knocked on the door and requested a word. Now, seated in front of the chief inspector, he clearly wanted more than a word, his stern expression speaking volumes.

It quickly turned into a fractious meeting as the DI plucked up courage to challenge the chief inspector, not a man known for his generosity when being asked by junior officers to justify decisions. Indeed, it was well known among the detectives in Western Division that only Colley among more junior officers had the kind of personal relationship with Blizzard that allowed him to take the prickly chief inspector to task without being reprimanded. Which is why the other detective constables and sergeants tended to use Colley as a communications channel when they had something on their mind that required Blizzard to re-think his decisions.

It was different for DIs. They were the next link down in the command chain from chief inspector and were expected to fight their own battles. As such, Chris Ramsey realized that only he could resolve the situation in which he found himself. He had tried to push the matter to the back of his mind and concentrate fully on the inquiry but the doubts just kept coming back, growing more insistent every time, gnawing away at him and demanding that he broach them with the chief inspector before the situation got out of all proportion. When it started to cloud his judgement, disturb his sleep and affect his mood so that his wife had begun to complain about how cranky he had become and how short he was with their young daughter, Chris Ramsey realized it was time to act. The news that Colley had been sent to Cumbria without the DI's knowledge was the final straw.

'I understand Colley went on a job out of area first thing?' said the DI.

'He did.' Blizzard's reply was cool.

'May I ask why?' asked Ramsey.

'I sent him to follow up a lead.'

'What was it, may I ask – and why was I not informed?'

'In case you had not noticed,' said Blizzard firmly, irritated by the accusing tone in the DI's voice, 'you report to me and not the other way round.'

'Can I speak freely?' asked Ramsey, his pursed lips testament to a man fighting to keep his emotions under control.

'I imagine you will, whatever I say.'

'I feel I have been left out of the loop on this one,' said Ramsey angrily, 'and it's not fair.'

'Explain,' said Blizzard calmly, knowing what Ramsey meant but wanting a little extra time to think before he responded.

The last thing he wanted to do was alienate his DI in the middle of such a high-pressure inquiry. Not that he needed much time to think; Blizzard had been expecting such an approach from Ramsey ever since the chief inspector had assumed control of the murder inquiry and recruited Colley to work as his right-hand man rather than asking the DI to help him. Ramsey was a thorough, dependable detective but his lack of faith in his own abilities, along with his lack of investigative flair, were the things in Blizzard's view which held back the DI as a police officer. Conversely, the opposite was true of the sergeant, whose ability to come up with new angles and show enough confidence to follow them through was the thing the chief inspector found appealing.

'I am a perfectly competent detective,' said Ramsey.

'Not in question,' nodded Blizzard. 'You would not be a DI in my division if you were not.'

Ramsey had to agree. Everyone remembered the last DI but one who was moved back into uniform when Blizzard decided that he was not up to the job. The DI had tried to win his job back but failed when Arthur Ronald backed his chief inspector right down the line. Last thing Ramsey heard, the old DI was a uniform inspector in the admin unit at headquarters, investigating paper clip allocations.

'After all, it was me who first drew attention to the

THE VENGEANCE MAN | 169

Vengeance Man,' said Ramsey tentatively, self-preservation jostling with anger.

'Granted and I have already acknowledged my initial error of judgement.'

'And I do not begrudge you taking over the murder inquiry....'

Blizzard's eyes flashed.

'I am sure Arthur Ronald will be delighted to hear that you approve of his decision to place me in charge,' he said sharply.

'I didn't mean it like that ... it's just that some things need to be said.'

'Yes, well be careful how you say them, Detective Inspector.'

The use of his formal title was not lost on the DI.

'Might I suggest you make your point,' said Blizzard, already knowing the reply.

'The point is this,' and Ramsey leaned forward and spoke earnestly. 'I should be your right hand man on this, not David Colley. He's a DS and I am a DI and....'

'Yes, you are the DI,' said Blizzard, cutting across him before he could get into his stride. 'But DIs are there not just because they are good detectives but because they are good managers as well. It's the same with chief inspectors. You know that, Chris. I spend more time doing sodding paperwork than out there doing something useful. And how much time do you spend out in the field these days?'

'Yes, but....'

'But nothing. You are like me, you spend more time than you should shuffling bloody bits of paper. But that's part of management, Chris. That is why I gave you the job of organizing the raids on all those criminals. That was a big responsibility and I needed a damned good manager of detectives to handle it. Colley could not do that. That is not his style.'

It happened not to be something Blizzard believed – Colley could rise to any challenge, he reckoned – but he sensed that a bit of soft-soaping was needed to defuse the tension. It did not work.

'Oh, so I am just some kind of glorified paper-pusher?' sniffed Ramsey.

'That is not what I am saying. What I am saying is that I needed someone to be able to pull it all together and I turned to you,' and Blizzard held up a bulky report listing details of interviews with the underworld figures they had hauled in for questioning over recent days. 'This is excellent work, Chris. Somewhere in here may be the bit of the jigsaw we are missing. The thing that leads us to Moody and Ransome, or Marty Cundall, or maybe even to the Vengeance Man. And even if it isn't, we have learnt so much from the interviews that there are enough leads on other crimes to keep us busy for six months.'

'I appreciate....'

'In fact,' and Blizzard was making it up as he went along now, impressing himself with the brilliance of his improvisation. 'When this is all over, I want to talk to you about planning a programme of operations based on the information you and the team have gleaned. The super likes the idea a lot.'

He must talk to Ronald as well, and quickly, he thought, to make sure he knew what to say when challenged by Ramsey. That was the problem with devising policy on the hoof, you had to make sure it didn't put noses out of joint. It would not do for Ronald to hear that he had agreed to a major operation with all the financial implications that came with it without having actually been consulted.

'We'll call it Operation Follow-up and you will be in sole charge,' continued Blizzard, ignoring the thought of Ronald's inevitable protestations about tying up manpower and incurring overtime costs.

'Really?' said Ramsey, cheering up and appearing to grow in stature, his shoulders less hunched.

'Oh, yes, this could be a big break for you, Chris,' and Blizzard held up the report. 'I am damned sure that Marty

Cundall is not the Vengeance Man but think of the kudos for Western Division – and for you – if we end up being the ones who prove his links to organised crime. Regional Crime Squad would be green with envy. They have been trying to lock him up for years. And who knows, a good result could even lead to an invite to be seconded to them.'

The DI considered the comment for a moment then shook his head. It sounded good but he was not fooled.

'Trying to get rid of me?' he asked plaintively.

'Of course not. I am just pointing out the opportunities this opens up for you in the future.'

'That's all very well but what about now, guv? I never get to accompany you....'

His voiced tailed off as he realized how ridiculous it sounded, and he gave the chief inspector a weak look. 'I guess I sound like a spoiled child?'

'No, you don't,' and Blizzard shook his head. 'You sound like a DI who thinks he should be a chief inspector, calling the shots. And there's nothing wrong with that. There would be a problem if you didn't think like that. But Chris, I know you think I prefer Colley to you. It is no secret that I think he should be a DI one day but not yet and not at your expense, Chris. You still have a job to do here.'

Ramsey seemed slightly mollified by the comment.

'Listen,' said Blizzard, 'we have all been under pressure during the past two weeks. When did you last have a day off?'

'It's true,' nodded Ramsey, suddenly aware that he felt very weary.

'And we don't think straight when we are tired.'

'That's true enough but if you are suggesting that I dip out....'

'No, no, of course not,' said Blizzard hurriedly. 'Besides, if I asked any of you to take a day off, I imagine you would all refuse.'

'Not until this is all sorted out,' said Ramsey firmly.

'Indeed. I am just saying that investigations like this put

pressures on all of us. The time to discuss this matter is when this inquiry is all done with and everyone is not so tired and is thinking more rationally.'

There was a tap on the door and Colley poked his head round the door, an excited look on his face.

'Which could be sooner that we think given the gleam in the sergeant's eye,' said Blizzard. 'How did you get back so fast?'

'I'm sure you'll stump up for the speeding tickets,' grinned Colley.

'I hope that's a joke,' grunted Blizzard. 'Let's see it then.'

'Now there's interesting,' breathed Blizzard, beaming as he scanned the document handed to him by the sergeant, then handed it to Ramsey. 'Gentlemen, I think we just took a big step towards wrapping this up. David, with me.'

As they reached the door and Ramsey headed off down the corridor, trying to conceal his disappointment at not being asked to go with them, Blizzard said, 'Chris, remember what I said.'

Ramsey turned, nodded and headed off to his office.

'What's that about?' asked Colley, pushing open a swing door as the officers headed in the opposite direction.

'Diplomacy,' and Blizzard tapped the side of his nose. 'Ronald would be proud of me.'

'John Blizzard and diplomacy,' chuckled Colley as they headed for the car park, 'whatever next?!'

'Watch it,' growled Blizzard. 'No one's indispensable.'

CHAPTER **TWENTY-TWO**

ater that afternoon, Bob Chatterton eyed the detectives uneasily over the interview room table. He had known something was wrong the moment they had arrived at his cottage and said they wanted to take him down the station. He realized to his horror that they had discovered the secret that he had tried to push to the back of his mind, and that he was to be made to relive one of the most humiliating – no, the most humiliating – experience of his life. Now, he sat on the same chair on which Robert Stanshall had sat but in an altogether less confident mood. His demeanour, darting eyes, hunched shoulders and clenched fists suggested a man struggling desperately to maintain some kind of control. And failing dismally.

'Bob, Bob' said Blizzard, sitting down and placing his plastic cup of tea on the desk, 'you really have been giving us the runaround.'

'I don't know what you mean,' replied Chatterton guardedly, perspiration glistening on his forehead and acutely aware of how hot he felt.

'Let's cut the pretence,' snapped Blizzard, 'I have three people in the mortuary....'

'Three?' asked the historian, surprised.

'Three,' repeated Blizzard, declining to elaborate on the comment, 'and throughout all of this you have been messing us around. That stuff about Stanshall was a red herring, wasn't it?'

'It was not!' protested Chatterton.

'Come on,' said Blizzard accusingly, 'you knew he was no more a killer than me. What motive would he have to kill off the very thing in which he planned to invest two million pounds?'

'I was trying to help,' said Chatterton weakly.

'Tell him sergeant.'

Colley leaned forward and placed the sheet of paper obtained that morning on the desk.

'What's that?' asked Chatterton uneasily.

'That,' said Colley, 'is the statement I took from Margaret Henderson this morning.'

'Who?' asked Chatterton failing to hide the look of recognition on his face.

'Don't try it on,' said the sergeant sharply. 'She was a supply teacher at Heston Comp when you were there.'

'I don't remember her,' said Chatterton defensively.

'But she remembers you,' said Colley with a wicked smile. 'Boy, does she remember you.'

Once they had discovered that Bob Chatterton had been a supply teacher at Heston Comp, Colley had gone back to the school to find out more. Nobody had mentioned his name before because they did not realize that the police were interested in him, and because his time there had been so brief that most of them had forgotten him anyway. When he jogged memories, however, one of the teachers pointed Colley in the direction of Margaret Henderson. Although they had had the information for some time, it had taken the sergeant time to find her because she had left the teaching profession and was now living in semi-retirement in a cottage on the Cumbrian coast. Things had been further confused because, having been divorced, she had reverted to her old surname. But he had found her in the end and before daylight, the sergeant had driven over to Cumbria and interviewed her in the trim little living room of her cottage before driving back, considerably faster than he had gone, desperate to show Blizzard what he had obtained.

'You see,' said Blizzard, 'the sergeant here did a bit of checking. How you got the posting at the school was easy, you told us that. You and Mervyn Howatch are big buddies but why you left....'

'You will recall,' said Colley, taking up the story, 'that you and Margaret used to sit together in the staff room. You were both supply teachers, which bonded you together. Indeed, you became good friends.'

Chatterton was staring at him with horror written all over his face. Eventually he admitted defeat and nodded dumbly.

'Margaret told me this morning,' said the sergeant, 'that contrary to what you told us, Eddie Barton and Roger Colclough were in your class.'

'Oh, God,' breathed Chatterton.

'And that they made your life hell. In fact, Mervyn Howatch once had to come into the classroom himself because there was so much noise. Isn't that right, Mr Chatterton?'

'Yes.'

The voice was hoarse, little more than a whisper.

'Tell me about that morning,' said Blizzard.

'They were out of control,' whispered Chatterton, transported back to a gloomy winter's morning at Heston Comprehensive School and a hopelessly idealistic, but weak, teacher standing before a class of unruly teenagers who had sensed the fear in his eyes.

Barton had been the first to react, hurling a history textbook at Chatterton when his back was turned as he wrote on the board. The book had struck him on the head and when he turned round, Barton and Colclough were laughing at him. There were plenty of decent kids in the class but they were intimidated by Barton and Colclough, bad lads and the magnet for a small group of disruptive pupils who had made Chatterton's life a misery during the previous few weeks, the stress growing so acute that he felt physically sick before going in to teach most mornings.

Losing his temper after the book struck, Chatterton had stormed down the classroom and confronted Barton, ordering him to leave the room and go to see the head-teacher, yelling at him that he would be expelled. Barton had leered at him, a grin that had haunted Chatterton down the years. He saw it in his nightmares, so much so that he had become frightened to go to sleep for months afterwards. And he saw it now again as he sat in that airless little interview room and felt once more that sick feeling in the pit of his stomach. He also heard once more Barton's taunting voice, challenging him to strike him, reminding him what happened to teachers who hit children.

'And what happened next?' asked Blizzard.

Tears welled up deep inside Chatterton and he hunched over the desk.

'Then he struck me,' he sobbed, and looked at the detectives with bemusement and disbelief on his face. 'He struck his teacher.'

Chatterton could feel the sting of the blow on his cheek yet.

'And after that?'

Chatterton shook his head.

'Mayhem. It was a riot, Chief Inspector. They were on the desk, shouting and hooting, throwing things around. A couple of them took their shirts off and waved them round their heads. It was awful. Mervyn heard the racket and came in and sorted it out – he can be a hard man can Mervyn – but that was it for me. I told Mervyn I wanted to leave. I couldn't take it any more. He didn't argue. How could he after what had happened? I went that day. I never taught again after that.'

And he turned glistening eyes on them.

'I only wanted to teach, Chief Inspector,' he whispered, 'that was all I wanted to do. Is there anything wrong with that?'

'No,' said Blizzard, feeling a sense of sympathy for the broken man sobbing in front of him. 'No, there isn't.'

'But it did not end there, did it?' asked Colley softly.

'They found my house a couple of days later,' said Chatterton in a low voice. 'Came round one night, all four of them. Barton and his cronies. I lived over on Mirebrook Lane in those days. I was in the living room reading a book when I heard them. I looked out and next thing I knew a brick came in through the window....'

'And then?'

'I ran out but they just laughed at me. Barton,' and his voice turned into a hiss, full of pent-up rage and anger, 'that little bastard, he laughed in my face. Next morning, when I came downstairs the garage had been broken into....'

His voice tailed off. The detectives let him recover his composure.

'I kept some of my history books there,' he said at length. 'No room left in the house. They had torn the pages out.'

He started to sob.

'Such beautiful books. So beautiful.'

'Did you tell the police?' asked Blizzard.

'No.'

'Why not?'

'It would only have made things worse if the lads thought I had told tales about them. They were a law to themselves.'

'Perhaps,' said Blizzard pointedly, 'if more people had done the right thing when this lot were kids all this might have been avoided. Well, now, Bob, it's time to put things right.'

Chatterton looked at him with a bemused expression on his face.

'I know what you're thinking,' he said, 'but I didn't kill them.'

'Why didn't you tell us about this then?' asked Colley, tapping the statement on the table. 'We were bound to find out sometime.'

'I was ashamed,' said Chatterton, and his voice was

laced with bitterness, 'how do you think it feels to know that you were forced out of your job by a bunch of teenagers? And yes, I am glad they are dead, and no, I don't care if Ransome and Moody die. But no, Sergeant, no I did not kill them. I don't have the guts for it.'

'But Mervyn might have,' said Colley calmly, adding in an echo of Chatterton's words. 'After all, he can be a tough man, can Mervyn'.

Chatterton looked at him sharply.

'Don't twist my words, Sergeant. Mervyn Howatch is a good man.'

'The game's up, Bob,' said Colley. 'Time to take us to him.'

Chatterton looked at him in amazement. Blizzard watched in admiration as his sergeant seized control of the interview, his energy electrifying the room.

'But I don't know where he is,' said Chatterton, the tone of voice defensive yet not convincing.

'Not a good idea to leave any skeletons in the cupboard,' said the sergeant, eyeing him shrewdly.

'I don't know what you are talking about.'

'Come on, Bob,' said Colley, his voice hardening. 'Kids are dying and we are sick of being messed about by people who should know better. We want Mervyn Howatch and we want him now. You know where he is and I would hate to have to charge you with perverting the course of justice.'

For a moment it looked as if Chatterton was about to say something then he nodded.

'OK,' he said. 'I'll tell you.'

A few minutes later, Colley left the room, followed by the chief inspector. Outside in the corridor, the sergeant leant his head against the wall and gave a sigh of relief.

'Excellent work, Sergeant,' said Blizzard delightedly, 'but how did you know that he was hiding Mervyn Howatch? For all we know, Mervyn Howatch is dead.'

'Call it instinct,' shrugged Colley.

'And that,' beamed Blizzard, patting him appreciatively on the shoulder, 'is why I ask for you and not Chris Ramsey on these little shindigs....'

CHAPTER **TWENTY-THREE**

I t was early evening and John Blizzard and David Colley were standing at the end of one of the rundown terraced streets on the fringes of the city centre, right on the edge of Western Division. A quarter of a mile away were the gleaming neon shopfronts and the bright lights of central Hafton, just starting to come back to life after the end of the working day and the departure of the office workers. Night-time drinkers headed noisily for happy hour in the pubs, young couples started to queue outside the cinema and taxis ferried the fags-and-curlers brigade to the large bingo hall.

But in Robson Street it was a different picture. Built in the Victorian age, and subsequently re-named in the mid-twenties in honour of a particularly prominent local alderman, Robson Street had now fallen on hard times. Once, people had been proud to live in Robson Street but over recent times, property landlords had snapped up the houses and turned them into what the council called homes of multiple occupation, but what everyone else called bedsit-land. Houses once warm and welcoming, which rang to the happy sounds of family life, were now shabby, silent, grim and dark. Where there had been gaily decorated children's bedrooms, were now poorly furnished bedsits, their carpets threadbare, the furniture, what there was of it, rickety and well past its best, the wallpaper peeling off the damp walls. Most of the bedsits were let out to DSS clients, some decent people among them but hugely outnumbered by the alcoholics, drug takers and scroungers who had moved in over recent years. Both gable ends of the street were blighted by vulgar graffiti, their crudely spray-painted messages testament to a street whose finery had long since been reduced to tatters and whose pride had long since gone. At least one of the houses had been raided by the Drugs Squad in the previous few weeks after a group of Jamaican dealers opened a crack house.

Standing at the end of the street as the fog started to roll across the city again, Blizzard and Colley felt a strange sense of satisfaction despite the uninspiring scene before them, illuminated by the only two street lights still working. Neither man put it into words but each realized instinctively that this was the world in which they felt most comfortable, the world in which they were supposed to function. Not for them the repressed world of the new housing estates, with their façades of respectability concealing dark secrets that would tear lives apart if anyone dared speak of them. No, here in Robson Street, for all its problems, was a certain honesty and a reality the detectives appreciated. Yes, it was ugly and depressing but you knew where you were in places like Robson Street, and both Blizzard and Colley realized with a start that during their time on the Vengeance Man inquiry they had missed it.

They were there because Bob Chatterton, misery compounded upon misery as he reluctantly betrayed his old friend, had told them that number eighteen was where Mervyn Howatch had been hiding out since his disappearance. Chatterton had gone to visit him several times, he admitted, taking food and toiletries as well as updating the headteacher on developments in the murder investigation. Now, Chatterton seemed relieved that the cloak-and-dagger life was over. Mervyn Howatch was someone else's problem now and Chatterton felt a great weight lifted from his shoulders. He had already done his duty as a friend. Howatch had done him a favour by getting him the supply teaching job at Heston Comp and by writing him a decent reference despite the humiliating events surrounding his departure, and Chatterton felt now that the debt was paid, that he could conceal what he knew about Mervyn Howatch's wherabouts no longer. His conscience, weighed down for so long, was clear. No skeletons left in the cupboard. Plenty of demons but no skeletons.

Blizzard had consulted with Ronald and decided that a low-profile approach was required – places like Robson Street could go funny if you got it wrong – so there was only him and Colley at one end of the street and, standing at the other, Chris Ramsey, delighted to be involved in the operation, and Sergeant Tulley. Dependable, reliable Tulley, the man to have in a crisis. But just in case he wasn't, Blizzard had taken the precaution of asking for uniform to provide a back-up unit, its burly officers parked out of view down a side alley in the crew bus, playing cards as they always did on such occasions, waiting for a call that so often never came. Such inactivity was often the lot of the tactical support officer.

'What do you think?' asked Colley as they stared down the deserted street.

'Seems quiet enough,' said Blizzard. 'Come on, let's get this over with.'

Number eighteen was a particularly neglected house, ragged green curtains in its front window, a gaping hole in the wall where the bell should have been and weeds scruffily poking their way through the front step. Blizzard took a deep breath and pushed the door, which swung open to reveal a long gloomy hallway.

'So much for home security,' he murmured, gesturing to Ramsey and Tulley to go round the back to cut off the escape route over the yard wall, then stepping inside. 'Remind me to get crime prevention to pay a visit.'

Colley chuckled in the darkness. The house was dank

THE VENGEANCE MAN | 183

and permeated by an unpleasant musty smell, a nose-wrinkling mixture of rotting wallpaper and crumbling plaster, the hallway illuminated by a lone unshaded light bulb. Stepping carefully to avoid the silverfish that darted across the linoleum, Blizzard and Colley edged their way towards the darkened stairs and started slowly to ascend into the shadows, feet clomping on the bare boards, hearts pumping as the darkness enveloped them. On the landing, the only light came from a crack beneath one of the doors and Blizzard could dimly make out the words Flat 3.

'This is it,' he said and knocked loudly.

'Who is it?' asked a nervous-sounding voice.

'Police,' said Blizzard.

A door across the landing swung open and a scrawny man dressed only in a vest and underpants and clutching a can of strong lager stepped out.

'Whoar you doing?' he asked in a drunken, aggressive voice.

'Arresting you if you don't shut up,' said Colley.

The man looked for a moment as if he was about to say something but one look at the lean sergeant changed his mind and, muttering oaths under his breath, he said nothing more and went back into his flat.

'I've always admired your respectful way of dealing with the public,' murmured Blizzard. 'You must teach me your secret one day.'

Colley beamed.

The door to number three opened and they were confronted by a tall man, in his early fifties, dressed in a tatty black T-shirt and stained jeans. His brown hair, was greasy and flattened down, and haunted eyes stared at them out of a gaunt unshaven face.

'Mervyn Howatch?' asked Blizzard.

The man looked at them bleakly.

'Yes,' he said in a voice that shook slightly as he surveyed the stern-faced officers.

'Well, my name is Detective Chief Inspector John

Blizzard and this is Detective Sergeant David Colley,' and he allowed himself the ghost of a smile. 'I think it's fair to say that we want a word with you....'

CHAPTER **TWENTY-FOUR**

Mervyn Howatch eyed the detectives anxiously as they sat in the interview room at Abbey Road Police Station later that evening. Having been given a shower, a change of clothes and a hot meal, he looked more human, more mentally composed, even if his eyes still betrayed the confusion and fear he was feeling. Blizzard couldn't help noticing with his usual fascination, the way the man's curly curly brown hair had frizzed up again, making him look like a mad scientist.

'I knew you'd come for me,' said Howatch. 'Bob Chatterton isn't terribly good at keeping secrets.'

'Where have I heard that before?' murmured Blizzard.

'Not fair on him really,' added Howatch.

'So what was the plan?' asked the chief inspector, handing him over a coffee in a plastic cup.

'Thank you,' said Howatch, taking a sip. 'Not sure there was one. I just needed to get away.'

'You've caused a lot of people a lot of trouble,' said the chief inspector. 'Your wife is desperately worried.'

'I appreciate that,' nodded Howatch, the voice trembling at the mention of his wife. 'It's strange, though. The longer you are out there, the harder it is to come back in. Then when Bob told me you reckoned I might have killed those boys, well, what could I do? Mind, I would have given myself up eventually.'

'So why go in the first place?' asked Colley.

'So many things,' said Howatch, shaking his head wearily, 'so many things.'

'Like?'

'Things were going badly at the school, the council had virtually admitted that they would close us down, and I knew that our Ofsted would be a disaster. I was working all the hours God gave but things weren't getting any better. The teaching staff were demoralized, the kids were demoralized, I was demoralized. I had lost the ability to lead the team. Can you understand that?'

'Personally, no,' said Blizzard, who thrived on such pressure and prided himself on never losing control in even the tightest of situations, 'but I can understand that it must have hurt a man like you.'

'And I became convinced I was ill,' said Howatch, a fearful look in his eyes. 'My mother died of cancer, Chief Inspector. I thought – think – that I have it as well. The headaches are terrible.'

He paused and there were tears in his eyes.

'Poor Janet,' he whispered, thinking of his wife again. 'Does she know I am here?'

'Yes,' nodded Blizzard. 'She's in one of our waiting rooms. You can see her later.'

'Thank you.'

The gratitude was heartfelt.

'But first I need some answers. Tell me about Barton and his pals.'

'Scum,' snorted Howatch, tears banished by the anger. 'Absolute scum. You know, I have been teaching for more than thirty years and I had never come across a child I couldn't turn to the good in some way. There was always at least one redeeming feature. But Barton? Nothing. Everything I tried just failed. The same with Colclough. They were the leaders, Chief Inspector. Moody and Ransome were followers who fell under their spell. At least at the start. By the end, they were all as bad as each other. The staff were frightened of them all. No one dared stand up against them. Sometimes I felt like I was the only one fighting the battle....'

'What about your deputy?' asked Colley.

'John Pendrie,' and Howatch gave a dry laugh. 'Too busy smoking his dope to care. You look like it doesn't surprise you, Sergeant?'

'I'd guessed,' said Colley.

'Oh, yes,' and the voice was scathing, 'John Pendrie liked his cannabis and the attention of the young girls in the sixth form. I could never prove it but I reckon he was selling it to them. We never got on. He never believed in discipline like I did.'

'He made that clear to us,' nodded Blizzard.

'I'll bet he did,' snorted Howatch. 'I bet he couldn't wait to jump into my seat. I imagine he'll have made dope compulsory by now.'

There was revulsion written on his face.

'And I'm sure he fancied Janet,' he added. 'I saw the way he looked at her.'

The detectives exchanged glances, recalling the way Pendrie had comforted her.

'Tell me about Bob Chatterton,' said Blizzard, changing the subject. 'He does seem to have an unhealthy fascination with John White. Could he be the Vengeance Man?'

'Oh, he's not your killer, Chief Inspector,' smiled Howatch, 'not Bob. He hasn't got it in him. Yes, he's bitter about what happened with Barton and the others, and I am sure he has not shed any tears about the dead boys, but he's not a killer.'

'He says it wrecked his teaching career,' said Blizzard. 'That sounds like a pretty powerful motive to me.'

'He wrecked his own career,' said Howatch dispassionately. 'He wasn't strong enough. Couldn't control a class. I'd already decided not to renew his contract when we had to let him go after the bust-up in the class-room.'

'Did he know that?'

'No. He had decided to go anyway. Why add to his misery?' and Howatch took a sip of his coffee.

'Tell me about your own interest in John Ignatius White,' said Blizzard.

'It was purely historical,' said Howatch calmly. 'I studied that period of history at university. Always said I would write a book about it when I retired,' and he gave a sour laugh. 'Bob was horrified when he heard it. Thought I'd steal his ideas. Silly man.'

'There are those who might wonder if your interest is more criminal than academic,' said Blizzard. 'You had plenty of reason to hate Barton and his cronies. Some might say that you dressed up to scare them off after they started selling the drugs and that things got out of hand. Maybe it was an accident, maybe you did not mean to kill Eddie Barton, maybe you simply lost your temper.'

Howatch considered the statement.

'I guess it fits,' he nodded.

'Particularly since we know you have a temper and once assaulted a pupil.' continued Blizzard. 'Maybe once you had killed Barton you had to silence the others in case they pointed the finger at you, maybe they knew you had arranged to meet him in the graveyard that night. Maybe you lured Colclough to the graveyard to silence him as well, hoping that the others would come.'

'One against three?' asked Howatch, eyeing the detectives shrewdly. 'Besides, I don't hide behind anything when I fight my battles. That afternoon when I saw them selling drugs at the school gate, I went out to confront them as the headteacher of Heston Comprehensive, not as some strange character in a big hat.'

'Fair enough,' nodded Blizzard, 'but it's a strange coincidence that you disappeared just as the Vengeance Man killed Eddie Barton.'

'Granted,' nodded Howatch, 'but it wasn't me, Chief Inspector.'

And he gave them a wry smile.

'I know I have a reputation for discipline – but it tends not to go as far as killing my pupils. Not good for business, the education authority tends to frown on it, particularly when rolls are already falling.'

'So, can you prove you were somewhere else at the time?' asked Colley.

Howatch shook his head.

'I am afraid not. After I abandoned the car the night I disappeared, I wandered for what seemed an age. I went along the derelict docks near Heston, slept in an old shed the first night. In the end I found my way to the bedsit.' And he shuddered at the memory. 'Never again....'

'Didn't you see anyone?' asked Colley. 'Anyone at all who can verify your story?'

'I am afraid not,' said Howatch then paused for a moment. 'Hang on though, there was someone. That Derek Stoddart chap.'

'Where did you see him?'

'When I was wandering along the docks on that first night. There's a hole in the fence over by the old jetty. I assumed that's how he got in.'

'What was he doing?' asked Colley.

'I assumed he was walking his dog,' shrugged Howatch. 'Frankly I did not hang around for long. No point disappearing if people see you.'

He gave a crooked smile.

'How did you recognize him?' asked Blizzard.

'His picture had been in the paper a few times. He was the one kicking up a fuss about those armed robberies. Anyway, Derek Stoddart should be able to verify that I was there. I am sure he saw me as I turned to walk the other way,' and he looked at them hopefully, 'my hair is pretty distinctive, you know.'

'It may be but I am afraid that Derek Stoddart is dead,' said Blizzard quietly. 'Died this afternoon.'

Howatch sat back in shock.

'Was it an accident?' he asked at length.

'No, he was shot in a robbery at his shop.'

'I didn't know,' said Howatch, deflating before their eyes, his one chance of proving his innocence slipping away, 'I haven't seen a paper for a few days. Bob did all my shopping but he hasn't been for a while. That's how I knew he was getting cold feet. I knew he'd give me away eventually.'

'What exactly was Derek Stoddart doing when you saw him?' asked Blizzard, his interest in this new turn of events well and truly aroused, the comment chiming with an ill-formed train of thought that had been developing for a day or two and that he had not yet shared with anyone.

'Like I said, I didn't take much notice. I think he was standing looking out at the river. He had a black bag over his shoulder as I recall.'

'But you definitely didn't approach him?'

'No, like I said, I needed to get away to get my head straight and the last thing I wanted was to get into conversation with someone like that.'

'Like what?' asked Colley sharply.

'Couldn't keep his mouth shut that one, it'd be all over the media the next morning, wouldn't it,' and Howatch chuckled grimly. 'Not exactly my idea of vanishing off the face of the earth for a few weeks.'

'Mr Howatch,' said Blizzard, standing up suddenly and taking the headteacher and the sergeant by surprise. 'I don't think you killed those boys and as far as I can see you have not done anything wrong. I'm going to release you.'

'I appreciate the gesture,' said Howatch, turning grateful, if surprised, eyes on the chief inspector.

'Just don't let me down,' said Blizzard, pointing a warning finger at him. 'I'll be back in a few minutes. In the meantime, I will get someone to bring Janet in to see you. I am sure you have a lot to talk about. David, I have a little job for you.'

Within a few minutes, Blizzard was in Ronald's office, addressing the superintendent, a gleam in his eye.

'Arthur, I think we know who the Vengeance Man is. Or rather, was.'

'Go on,' said Ronald with a gleam in his eyes.

'Derek Stoddart.'

'Based on?'

'We assumed – not unreasonably given all the turmoil – that the killings of Barton and Colclough were something to do with the school. What if my initial gut instinct about the shooting of Stoddart was right, all along? What if it was an execution and they simply took the money because the opportunity was there? What if Ransome and Moody knew he was the Vengeance Man and came looking for him?'

'To avenge their mates?'

'Yes. I dismissed the idea early on, admittedly, but only because what we were finding out about Mervyn Howatch and Bob Chatterton made them look pretty decent suspects. Both had half-decent motives.'

'Yes, but what if Howatch said he saw Stoddart to throw us off the scent?' asked Ronald. 'We only have his word that he did not know Stoddart had been shot. What if he had heard that Stoddart was not likely to live – there's been enough about in the papers – and saw it as an ideal way of blaming someone else. What if it is Chatterton after all?'

'No, I can't see that,' and Blizzard shook his head. 'I think Mervyn Howatch is right about him, he's too much of a coward. Besides, Colley has checked his alibis for the nights of the killings and they all check out.'

'OK, but why would…?'

He got no further because Colley walked in to the superintendent's office.

'Good news,' he said with a grin as he sat down. 'Derek Stoddart doesn't have a dog.'

Ronald looked baffled.

'Howatch said the only reason he could think for Derek Stoddart being on the docks was because he was walking his dog – some local people go through the hole in the fence.'

'Maybe he just wanted to look at the river, like Howatch said,' said Ronald. 'You do.'

'Maybe,' admitted Blizzard, 'but what if he hid his Vengeance Man gear there?'

'Sergeant?' asked Ronald turning his gaze at Colley. 'Any thoughts?'

'I'll buy it,' nodded Colley.

There was a knock on the door and Chris Ramsey walked in.

'Got something for you,' he said excitedly.

'Go on,' said Blizzard, gesturing to the DI to sit down.

'One of my informants has confirmed that Barton and his mates definitely were the shop robbers. He says they wanted to move into big-time drug dealing, make their money and go to live in Spain. Ransome's father owns a villa out there apparently. My informant says they had been negotiating to buy a big shipment of heroin but didn't have enough money. That's why they were robbing so many shops – because time was running out and the consignment is due. The guys they are buying it from are Dutch – Amsterdam-based apparently – and our lot were terrified of what they would do if the drugs turned up and they didn't have the cash ready.'

'Really,' whistled Blizzard, 'now that is interesting.'

'So, I checked with Regional Crime Squad and our drugs boys and they had both heard about a big shipment due to come in over the next few days but they didn't know who was behind it,' and he grinned, something they did not often see Chris Ramsey do. 'They thought it was coming in at Hull! If the truth be told, I reckon they were pretty pissed off that we knew where and who and they didn't.'

'That's your transfer to them off,' quipped Blizzard.

'What – and miss working with you lot,' said Ramsey with a wry smile.

Blizzard beamed, and winked at his sergeant.

CHAPTER **TWENTY-FIVE**

With Mervyn Howatch and Bob Chatterton ruled out of the inquiry, Abbey Road Police Station was a hive of activity the next morning as Blizzard presided over a review of the information that his detectives had gleaned about Derek Stoddart over the past few days. Everything they had discovered confirmed that he was intensely angered at the attacks on his shops, and particularly the robbery that had rendered his wife so deeply traumatized, but whether he was angry enough to kill was another matter. His claim that he had declined Marty Cundall's help, a story supported by other shopkeepers who described him as a moderating influence amid their fury, had all but convinced the chief inspector that he was not the type to kill. Now it seemed to have been a highly effective smoke-screen.

Blizzard cursed himself; by looking at Marty Cundall they had studied the wrong side of the conversation outside the school that night. Stoddart was the one they should have concentrated on. In an attempt to find out more, Colley had that morning conducted a brief interview with Stoddart's wife but found that she had withdrawn so far into herself that little of use could be gleaned from her whispered answers. Leaving the nursing home where she had been temporarily housed since the shooting of her husband, he could see why Derek Stoddart was so enraged at what had happened to her. But for all that, and hard as they looked, the detectives could come up with nothing to link him to the Vengeance Man attacks. Suspicion was one thing, Blizzard reminded his detectives, proof was another.

'Dammit, I'm sure it's there,' said Blizzard more than once as he sifted through the sheafs of paper strewn across his desk. 'Any word from the search team?'

'Nothing,' said Colley, sitting opposite him and flicking idly through another report from one of the team.

Chris Ramsey had been leading a team of detectives and uniformed officers searching the derelict docklands near Heston, picking their way through the murk since early morning. It was a monumental task because the docks had once covered a vast area. In their heyday, they had been home to the towering cranes and clanging shipyards on which Hafton had forged its prosperity but these days they lay derelict, huge areas of twisted metal, tumbledown buildings, disused railway lines and a rusting hulk that once plied the high seas but now lolled on an abandoned slipway. Painstakingly, Ramsey and his team picked their way through the debris of the area's industrial past for hours, checking every building, every nook and cranny for signs that Derek Stoddart had been there.

Colley had been busy as well. After the sergeant left the nursing home, he and Tulley had re-searched Derek Stoddart's house, seeking something, anything, that might link the dead shopkeeper to the murderous attacks on Eddie Barton and Roger Colclough. Now, having drawn a blank, he was losing hope as he sat in Blizzard's office, sifting through the documents they had seized. Which was when he noticed the link they had been searching for. It was the telephone bills that gave it away, that and Stoddart's passion for meticulous record-keeping. It was the businessman in him.

With mounting excitement, the sergeant noticed that the same number occurred regularly. Not saying anything, he walked through into the CID room and checked with the phone company; it turned out to be a phone box in Heston. Colley jotted down the address then, deep in thought and recalling a scrap of conversation lodged in the recesses of his mind, put a call into Lincolnshire Police. It was a long shot but sometimes they pay off. This was one of those times. A few more phone calls, including one to Mervyn Howatch, confirmed his suspicions and with heavy heart and even heavier step, Colley walked back to the chief inspector's office.

'Where did you get to?' asked Blizzard, with a weary smile, tossing the report he was reading on to his desk.

'Checking something out.'

'You know, despite all these dead ends, I still have this feeling that we are finally on the right track with Stoddart,' said Blizzard. 'Hey, what's wrong?'

His voice tailed off as he saw the expression on his sergeant's face.

'We are.'

'Come again?'

'I don't think he was working alone,' said the sergeant, and handed over a piece of paper on which was written a single name. 'I think there are two Vengeance Men!'

'This has to be some kind of joke,' exclaimed Blizzard angrily, 'and a bloody bad one at that!'

'No joke, guv,' said Colley, sitting down. 'I wish it was. But the phone bills link him with Stoddart.'

'Oh, come on, there has to be a rational explanation.'

'I think there is,' said Colley grimly.

Over the next few minutes, the sergeant outlined a story that was as powerful as it was disturbing, and that provided the Vengeance Man with all the motivation any man could ever need. At the end of it, Blizzard sat back in his chair and stared out of the window. It was raining and the clouds were closing in. Colley walked quietly from the room, leaving the chief inspector staring out at the darkening storm clouds gathering. Blizzard could not remember when he had felt more alone.

CHAPTER **TWENTY-SIX**

B lizzard could feel his heart pounding as he crouched in the stairwell of the block of flats and listened to the familiar noises around him, the rustling of uniform, the click of firearms, the breathing of fellow officers. Behind him Colley waited impatiently, keen for the action to start. They were there because, just as Blizzard and the sergeant were about to head out to investigate Colley's new lead that morning, the sergeant had received an important call from one of his informants. The man, a low-level drug dealer, had conquered his fear and had come through with an address for Ransome and Moody. Trouble was, of all the addresses that the informant could have chosen, this was the worst of the lot and Blizzard and Ronald groaned when they heard it. They were going to raid the Spur.

The Spur was the worst council housing estate in the city, constructed around three large quadrangles, bordered on all sides by flats, many with boarded up windows. Broken bottles, used condoms and syringes littered the quadrangles and weeds poked through the cracks in the concrete. The blocks were terribly run-down, the concrete cracking, the paintwork peeling, many of the doors splintered and gashed, and threatening graffiti scrawled across many of the walls. As for the residents, there were one or two decent ones sticking it out against the tide of villainy despite intense intimidation but, for the most part, the occupants were pondlife, drug dealers, petty criminals, alcoholics, swirled together to make a soup of hopeless humanity living by its own amoral rules.

Blizzard hated the Spur and he hated the vast majority of its occupants but most of all he hated the way it had been allowed to get into this state. The chief inspector was clear on the causes for its decline and had caused furore at one meeting with council officials when he blamed them for neglecting the estate, pointing to the lack of investment and the inadequate tenancy scrutiny system, which had allowed the drug dealers to move in and force the decent people out. The council had submitted an official complaint against him – not their first, it would not be the last – but once again Ronald offered strong support and the matter blew over. However, Blizzard was not blind and readily acknowledged that it was not all the council's fault, a point he made in the meeting but the enraged council officials seemed to have forgotten.

The detectives admitted that there had been police failings as well. Indeed, they themselves had railed against the chief constable's calls for a softly-softly approach on the estate following a riot some months before in which three police officers were injured by slabs of concrete hurled from upstairs galleries. Blizzard and Ronald disliked the policy and disliked the impotence it brought to the police, which was why whenever they could find good reason they sent detectives on to the estate to make arrests. And there was good reason indeed this time.

Once he heard the address, Ronald had called in uniform support and the firearms team. This was going to be tricky and it made sense to have the muscle and the firepower on their side. Now, shortly after noon, the hurried planning over, the officers were edging their way up the stairwell of one of the blocks, wrinkling their noses at that acrid smell of stale urine that characterized the Spur. Already, there were stirrings on some of the upper landings, the occupants alerted by their look-outs to the convoy of police vehicles that had just driven into the middle of the main quadrangle.

Ronald, who was in the centre of the quadrangle with Ramsey, had immediately liaised with the senior uniform officer on the scene, a superintendent for whom he had the greatest respect, and uniforms had fanned out rapidly across the quadrangle. They did nothing more for the moment; the last thing the police wanted was another riot during which their quarry could make good their escape.

'Let's get this over with,' hissed Blizzard to the firearms team as he crouched in the stairwell. 'The natives are getting restless.'

'OK,' said the officer.

Blizzard could see the whites of his eyes.

'Let's go,' said the firearms officer and within seconds his team was scuttling across the landing towards the flat named by Colley's informant. There was a lot of shouting and the rending sound of a door being sent crashing off its hinges, more shouting and a yell of 'drop it!' then the call of 'all clear'. Blizzard heaved a sigh of relief and walked out on to the landing, watching with grim satisfaction as a scruffy teenager, dressed in jeans and dirty white T-shirt, his hair dirty and lank, face unshaven, eyes flashing livid with hatred, was dragged out of the flat, protesting loudly all the time. Behind him walked a couple of firearms officers, holding up a couple of shotguns they had seized.

Blizzard walked up to the teenager and looked at him in silence for several seconds. The boy glared at him and tried to struggle free to get at the chief inspector. Blizzard smiled a thin, chilling smile.

'Good afternoon, Raymond,' he said. 'I'm your vengeance man!'

CHAPTER **TWENTY-SEVEN**

The interview with Raymond Ransome went badly right from the start, the teenager making it clear amid foul profanities-a-plenty that he had no respect for the police, or anyone else in authority for that matter. Blizzard and Colley sat in mounting horror as they witnessed the performance of a young man who had only been at school three years before. They recalled the old primary school pictures they had seen of him, of a cherubic freckly boy with a cheeky grin and wonky teeth, and found themselves deeply disturbed at the transformation that had been wrought by the drugs he was taking and the people with whom he was mixing.

But he was not so hard and tough as he imagined and after a couple of hours he started to wilt under the pressure from the grim detectives, calming down, moderating his language and beginning to answer their questions. Gradually, the detectives began to detect that beneath the tough exterior was a frightened and bewildered young man and although they were not particularly informative answers they were answers for all that. Blizzard sensed that, with him talking at last and freed from the influence of his partners in crime and the security they offered, the time was close for a breakthrough. At first it seemed he was wrong.

'Where's Paul Moody?' asked Blizzard again as he stared at Ransome across the desk in the interview room.

'Like I said, I ain't sayin' nuffin' to youse about Paul,'

said Ransome, glaring at the chief inspector and his sergeant. 'I ain't getting him in trouble with the filth.'

'I'd be obliged if you did not call us filth,' replied Blizzard calmly. 'Besides, he may be in a damned sight more than trouble with the police. He may be in danger of losing his life. The psycho who got your mates is still out there somewhere.'

'You reckon?' leered Ransome.

'If by that you are alluding to what you and Paul did to Mr Stoddart, it is not that simple,' said Blizzard.

Confusion flickered on Ransome's face.

'You see,' said Blizzard. 'We think the Vengeance Man is still out there – and so is your mate Paul. At least you're safe.'

'Call this safe!' spat Ransome, trying not to show his unease. 'Call a long stretch in prison safe?'

'At least no one will try to kill you if you keep your nose clean,' said Blizzard calmly. 'We may be the only ones who can prevent Paul from being murdered. Where is he?'

Ransome looked as if he were about to spit out another answer but the chief inspector's words seemed to have an effect and he was silent for a moment or two then looked at the detectives and nodded in defeat.

'I ain't seen Paul since last night,' he said.

'What happened?'

'He got a call,' said Ransome guardedly. 'On his mobile.'

'A call?'

'From a smack-head – in Heston.'

'The same one that called Roger Colclough?'

There was a pause then a nod.

'Who was he?' asked Blizzard.

'All I know is he knew the Vengeance Man or whatever he calls himself.'

'And what did the druggie say? How did he get Roger there?'

'Said this bloke wanted to talk over what happened to Eddie in the graveyard. We told Roger not to be so stupid but he went all the same. Said he had to end it once and for all.'

'Why did he go alone?'

'We said we should all go, said it would be safer that way, but he said we had to stay behind. Said it didn't make sense if we was all killed.'

'And last night?'

'Same thing,' shrugged Ransome.

'To meet at the graveyard again?'

'No, the waste ground next to the Rec in Heston.'

'Where you buy your guns,' said Colley, exchanging glances with Blizzard. They feared what they would find.

'I ain't sayin' nuffin' about guns.'

'Don't need to,' said Blizzard. 'We know all about your little games. Getting back to last night, you knew what had happened to the others, why didn't you go with him? Safety in numbers, surely?'

'I ain't answering that either.'

'I assume it was because one of you had to stay home in case word came in about your big drugs shipment,' said the chief inspector in an off-hand way.

Ransome started at the revelation that the police knew about the plan but quickly recovered his composure.

'See,' said Blizzard calmly. 'The game's up, Ray.'

'I ain't saying nuffin' else.' said Ransome defiantly. 'I've said too much.'

'Just one more thing,' said Colley, his mind suddenly going back to the night of Eddie Barton's death and a cowering teenager beneath a dripping tree. 'This druggie who passed on your messages from the Vengeance Man, I don't suppose by any chance that it was Billy Thompson?'

Ransome gaped at him.

'How the…?' he blurted out.

'Thank you,' said Colley, looked at the impressed Blizzard and winked.

'Instinct,' he said.

CHAPTER **TWENTY-EIGHT**

It did not take the police long to track down Billy Thompson – arrested in the litter-strewn bedsit where he lived – and it did not take him long to confess all. Sitting in the airless interview room and confronted by two stern-faced police officers, the dishevelled staring-eyed teenager was too frightened to do anything else. There was none of Raymond Ransome's defiance. Instead he sat trembling, eyeing the officers fearfully.

'So, how did you meet the Vengeance Man?' asked Blizzard. 'He's hardly the kind of chap you might bump into down the pub.'

'It was the night Eddie died,' said Thompson in a hoarse whisper. 'I lied about what he said to me. He caught me up as I tried to get out of the graveyard. It were scary. He said he would pay me good money if I passed on messages to the others.'

'How did you know where they were?'

'I'd got their mobile phone numbers,' said Thompson, explaining, 'they were the ones as sold me drugs if Eddie wasn't around.'

'Why didn't you tell us this earlier?' asked Blizzard.

'You seen what the Vengeance Man does to folks he don't like,' said Thompson. 'He freatened me, said I'd get the same as the others.'

And he shuddered.

'Sorry, Mr Blizzard, but you just ain't nearly as scary as he is.'

'Don't you believe it,' murmured the Chief Inspector. 'Do you know who he was?'

'Yeah.' nodded Thompson. 'That Stoddart fellow.'

'So who asked you to pass on the message last night?' asked Colley.

'Dunno,' and Thompson gave a vigorous shake of the head. 'The voice on the phone were different. I hadn't heard it before.'

'Unfortunately,' said a grim-faced Blizzard, standing up and pushing his chair back with a scraping sound. 'We have....'

As he headed out into the corridor, case proved, a disembodied voice spoke over his radio.

'Message from Control for Chief Inspector Blizzard,' it said. 'Please proceed to the waste ground off Ratcliffe Road in Heston where a body has been found by your search team.'

CHAPTER **TWENTY-NINE**

L ess than half an hour later, John Blizzard was standing on the wasteground behind the recreation centre, turning his coat collar up against the driving rain and staring bleakly at the body before them. Like the others, Paul Moody had died a horrible death. Lying in thick vegetation beneath several straggly trees, he was twisted grotesquely across a rusty old barrel, which had been dumped some time ago. His legs were splayed, the jeans spattered with mud, and his windcheater was caked in the blood that had spurted from the chest when his attacker had plunged the metal spike deep into his body. A quick glance around revealed that, for all it had been a well-planned murder, the victim lured to his death, it was a weapon of opportunity, one of the rusted fence posts piled up in the corner next to the perimeter wall. Echoes of Roger Colclough.

'Come on,' said Blizzard bleakly. 'Time to pick our man up.'

It was with heavy heart that Blizzard drove them through the streets of Hafton. The mid-afternoon gloom was closing in and, after a brief respite, the rain was beginning to fleck the windscreen again as he and Colley headed for the house. On their way, they passed the white pick-up truck driven by David Prendergast, piled high with rolls of turf. Prendergast waved cheerily at them and Blizzard smiled and waved back. Colley looked quizzically at Blizzard but the chief inspector shook his head.

'Plenty of time for that,' he said quietly. 'I want to make sure you're right first.'

'I am,' said Colley.

'Just let me play it my way,' said Blizzard, and he looked at the sergeant. 'Please.'

Colley shrugged.

'As long as you know what you're doing....'

Within a few minutes, they had drawn up outside the house and were walking up the short drive. Colley noticed idly that the borders had just been weeded. Everything in its right place and nice and tidy, he thought. On the face of it, the house was like every other one in the street, on the estate, in the village – and like so many of them it harboured a secret. A dark, wicked secret.

The door was opened by Albert Prendergast, whose face creased in a smile when he saw the chief inspector but clouded over when he saw the expression on the detective's face.

'Is something wrong?' he asked uneasily.

'Where was David going?' asked Blizzard curtly.

'He's got a client over in Burniston. He's got his mobile, do you want me to contact him?'

The voice was easy and charming as ever but the eyes betrayed unease.

'No, I am sure you can help us,' said Blizzard quietly. 'Tell us about Oliver, please.'

The blood drained from Albert Prendergast's face and he staggered backwards. Colley stepped forward to prevent the old man falling over and gently helped him into the living room. Once they had made him a cup of hot, sweet tea and settled him down in an armchair, Blizzard looked at him and repeated the question.

'So, please, Albert, tell me about Oliver.'

The old man turned haunted eyes on him.

'I always suspected,' he said in a hoarse whisper.

'Suspected what?'

Albert Prendergast's face assumed a dreamy far-off

expression as his mind was transported back in time, to a sunny garden in which played two small boys in shorts, one with blond curly hair, the other with dark straight hair. Happy, cheerful boys, dressed in Manchester United football strips, kicking a football around with their father and their grandfather, laughing and shrieking with joy. His mind switched to bedtimes, a doting grandfather reading stories to the boys, wonderous tales of dragons and brave knights, listened to with wide eyes as they lay tucked up in bed in rooms decorated with posters of star footballers and littered with toys. They were scenes of such unbearable innocence but consigned now to a dim and distant past, a different world that no longer existed. And as he remembered those happy, happy days, Albert Prendergast broke down and cried like he had never cried before.

The detectives let him cry and after a few minutes, he looked up at them with rheumy eyes.

'He was an angel, Mr Blizzard, an absolutely angel. Him and his brother.'

'Do I assume Daniel is at school at the moment?'

Prendergast nodded.

'When will he be back?' asked Blizzard.

'Six-ish. It's football practice.'

'Let him have a few more hours of innocence,' said Blizzard, the pain etched on his face. 'So tell us about Oliver.'

Albert paused then started to tell his story, each word taking an age to form.

'The family lived in Lincolnshire. He went to a comprehensive school over there. His mum died of cancer when he was eleven,' and Albert shook his head, 'such a shattering blow, she was a beautiful woman and a wonderful mother. Daniel seemed to cope with the loss better than Olly. I think younger ones do. Everything seemed to be going so well then one day, towards the middle of his third year I think it was, the school rang, said Olly had been caught with cannabis. Of course, there was a big investigation and Olly was expelled for a week.'

And his voice tailed off.

'We thought it was all sorted,' and his voice broke, 'but it turned out that he hadn't stopped taking drugs at all. Just kept taking them secretly. Then we heard that he had been given heroin by someone, another pupil they always reckoned, but they never caught him. Olly was expelled again.'

'What did David do?'

'What can a father do? He tried everything but Olly would not listen to any of us,' and again there was a shake of the head. 'Not even me, Chief Inspector. I reckoned that even if he wouldn't talk to his father he would speak to his grandfather. We had always got on so well but he just looked straight through me. If Daniel knew what was happening he never let on. They were very close, would do anything for each other. The school let Olly back in but it didn't work and he got himself expelled again for stealing from other children to pay for his drugs.'

'And then what happened?' asked Blizzard softly, knowing the answer.

'It was two days after his fourteenth birthday,' said Prendergast, mind transported back to that awful time. 'Olly was found....'

And again his voice faded. It was some moments before he could speak again. Eventually, he composed himself, gratefully accepting a glass of water brought into the darkening living room by the sergeant.

'Olly was found dead. It was just after four that the police officer came round to the house. I'll never forget it. We were visiting them for a few days. It was an afternoon like this, dark, so dark,' and he paused for a moment before resuming his story. 'The door bell rang. The police officer said Olly had been found lying on some wasteland not far from the school. The police reckoned he had taken an overdose by accident. Fourteen, Chief Inspector,' and he turned those haunted eyes towards the detective again. 'He was just fourteen.'

There was silence in the room and as the winter afternoon gloom closed in and the room darkened even further,
the detectives were acutely aware of the ticking of the clock
on the mantelpiece, something they had not noticed before.
Albert Prendergast sat, hunched, body wracked with his
sobbing.

Eventually Blizzard reached out and placed a hand on
his shoulder.

'I am sorry to have to ask you to relive this, Albert,' he
said softly. 'But I need to resolve this once and for all. The
killing has to stop.'

Prendergast looked up and nodded, pulling himself
together with an immense effort.

'I know. I know,' and he smiled weakly. 'It's time for it to
come to an end.'

'What happened after Olly's death?'

'The police investigated but they never found out who it
was. The school expelled a couple of boys but only for a
few days then they were back. Daniel's three years younger
and he had just started at the same school when we heard
that the boys were selling drugs again. David had no confidence in anyone at the school to stop it – and the police had
not done anything – so he moved his business up here.
He'd done some work in Hafton. He said it was a new start.
And for a while it was.'

'And then Eddie Barton?' said Blizzard.

Prendergast nodded.

'Daniel came home a few weeks ago and said Barton and
his gang were hanging around Heston selling drugs.
They'd offered drugs to some of his classmates. David was
terrified. It brought back so many bad memories. The fears
ran deep, Chief Inspector. He went to the school to try to do
something about it but nothing seemed to happen. He was
terrified it was all going to happen again.'

'So what did he do?'

Albert Prendergast looked him in the eye.

'I think you know, Chief Inspector. He was the

Vengeance Man. Him and that Stoddart fellow. Nasty man. I didn't like him at all. I kept telling David it was wrong and that he should steer clear of him but he wouldn't listen. He wasn't thinking straight. It was like he was under Stoddart's spell. David just couldn't stop himself. Ironic really.'

'Ironic?'

'It was like a drug.'

The significance of the comment was not lost on the detectives.

'So how come he hooked up with Stoddart?' asked Colley. 'They hardly seem the type to be friends.'

'David had done some work for him, relaid his lawn or something, then they met again at the quoits club a few weeks back. Got talking. David told him about Olly and Stoddart told him about his wife. David came home saying that society had gone to rack and ruin. Said he had to do everything in his power to protect Daniel from going the same way as Olly and that if no one else would do anything then he would. Said Derek Stoddart had the right idea.'

'So it was Stoddart's idea?' asked Blizzard keenly, seeing a way in which perhaps David's role was less pronounced.

'Thank you for the thought, Chief Inspector,' said Prendergast, reading his mind, 'but I think David was just as determined to press ahead with their plan.'

Prendergast shook his head again.

'I told him to go to the police,' he said, 'but David said they had failed Olly and Stoddart's wife and they were not going to fail Daniel. He hated the police for failing Olly. You were the only one he ever said anything nice about.'

'Much good it has done me,' murmured Blizzard gloomily. 'So that was when they dreamt up the Vengeance Man?'

Prendergast nodded.

'David said he had already gone on a business trip to Liverpool and got the black coat and the hat there so that no one would link it with events in Heston. Said the idea was to terrify the drug takers so the message would get back to Barton and his mates. They took turns to appear as John White. I think David quite enjoyed it at first. He was always one for the amateur dramatics when he was younger.'

'I assume they hit on the story because David heard about it from you?'

'Yes. I thought it was odd at the time.' The voice was getting stronger. 'David didn't have much interest in history but a few weeks after Chatterton's talk he started asking me about it. He was fascinated. I think David thought you would look at Bob Chatterton or Mervyn Howatch as a suspect. After all, David wasn't even at the meeting, was he? And he knew that Bob Chatterton and Mervyn Howatch had good reason to hate Barton and the others.'

'How?' asked Blizzard.

'He had a friend at the school. A teacher, I think.'

'Was the idea to kill Eddie Barton, do you know?'

'No,' and Prendergast shook his head vehemently. 'On the night it happened, David went expecting to find one of the drug takers but Barton was still there. When he got back I could see that something had gone wrong. David said Barton had taunted him, said he was going to sell heroin to Daniel. David said he lost control, grabbed the first thing that came to hand and hit him with it. He was in a terrible state when he got home.'

'And Colclough?'

'That was Stoddart. It was like he wanted one as well. He persuaded David to go along with it by saying that drugs were still being sold in Heston. Said Daniel was still not safe. That they might as well kill them all as stop at one. I'm not sure how but he lured Colclough to the graveyard and killed him as well.'

'And now Paul Moody is dead as well,' said Blizzard. 'David must have killed him.'

Prendergast turned sad eyes on him but said nothing.

'They were all killed using immense force,' said Blizzard. 'Could David really do that?'

'If he is filled with enough hate and anger,' said Prendergast softly, 'a man can do anything, Chief Inspector. I don't know about Stoddart but David was filled with enough hate for a dozen men. If you want a motive, you won't find a more powerful one than a parent's urge to protect a child, Mr Blizzard.'

And he turned those haunted eyes on Blizzard once more. Returning the gaze, the chief inspector could feel the anger and the pain, could feel the anguish and the fury, could feel them boring deep into his soul. And he knew then that anything was possible.

CHAPTER **THIRTY**

Darkness had fallen as John Blizzard sat in his office a couple of hours later, waiting for the call. Everything about Albert Prendergast's son's story had checked out and Mervyn Howatch, now released and recovering back home, had confirmed that Daniel's friends had been offered drugs by Barton. Daniel had not, according to the headteacher, taken any of the drugs but Howatch recalled his father being very angry when he heard the news. There had been a fractious exchange in the headteacher's office. Howatch had not thought to mention it because it was one of a number of similar meetings with furious parents demanding action be taken.

Having confirmed the story, Blizzard had issued a bulletin urging officers to keep an eye out for the pick-up truck, reasoning that an unsuspecting David would not realize they knew his secret. That is why he had waved cheerily at him when they passed him in his pick-up truck. In hindsight, that was a mistake.

After leaving Albert Prendergast, Blizzard and Colley headed round to the client's house in Burniston only to discover that David had only just left. Blizzard reasoned that David would head home but a patrol car driving through the estate on an unconnected inquiry seemed to have spooked their target, who drove off at high speed. The penny had dropped and Blizzard cursed himself for not arresting him earlier.

What David could not have known was that Ramsey's

search team on the docks had been at work all day and just
before five o'clock with the light – and hope – starting to
fade, the DI made the call John Blizzard had been waiting
for. Within twenty minutes, he and Colley were standing
by a ramshackle shed in one of the farthest flung corners of
the docks, the opposite end to which Mervyn Howatch
said he had seen Derek Stoddart on the night of the headteacher's disappearing act.

'Show me,' said Blizzard.

The uniformed officer opened the creaking door to the
shed and flashed his torch in the far corner. In among the
old tools and rusted boxes, they could clearly see a hole
hollowed out in the wall. Peering closer, they could just
make out a cavity containing a wide-brimmed black hat
and a neatly folded black coat.

'What now?' asked Colley.

'Endgame,' said Blizzard grimly. 'Once he knows we are
on to him, he will want to get rid of the gear.'

It was just after seven thirty that their man came, picking
his way tentatively through the debris towards the shed,
illuminating his way with a torch, the pinprick of light
growing stronger as he approached. It was very dark on
the old docks and the only other light was provided by a
pale moon, which was occasionally concealed behind the
ragged, scudding clouds. Blizzard and Colley, and the
other officers hiding around the site, watched with baited
breath as the figure approached. As he neared, they could
see him darting anxious looks to right and left and heard
his feet crunching across the wasteland. He arrived at the
shed and disappeared inside.

'Wait for it,' hissed Blizzard. 'I want him bang to rights.'

Moments later, the man emerged carrying the coat and
the hat.

'Evening, David,' said Blizzard calmly, stepping out of
the shadows and shining a torch in the startled man's
direction.

With a horrified cry, Prendergast leapt back and hurled

himself over an old chemical barrel, screaming out as the rusty metal bit into his leg, then started running for all his life towards the river, pursued across the small patch of wasteland leading to the habour by the officers, Colley leading the chase, all those hours building up fitness on the rugby field paying off. The chase went on for some minutes as Prendergast threw himself crazily over obstacles, hurdling scrap metal, diving in between rolls of wire metal and through gaps between some of the old workmen's store sheds. Eventually, just a few metres ahead of his pursuers, he squeezed through a gap in the fence and ran, still pursued by the officers, towards Heston harbour. Colley and one of the uniformed officers were leading the way, the wheezing Blizzard bringing up the rear. In the distance they could hear sirens and as they reached the harbour, could see flashing blue lights appearing at the end of the approach road.

Breathing hard, Prendergast ran along the paved path alongside the harbour wall, past the pleasure vessels and the fishing boats bobbing on the water down below him, his footsteps reverberating in the night air, his fleeing frame silhouetted by the moon, which had emerged from behind the clouds. Finally, he reached the end of the jetty and looked down desperately, seeing only the dark waters of the Haft, surging and eddying as they lapped against the harbour. As Colley and the uniformed constable ran towards him, he held up his hand wearily. For a few moments he stood in silence then noticed John Blizzard struggling along the harbour and gave a thin smile.

'Age seems to be catching up with your chief inspector,' he said, the voice slightly tremulous with the exertion of the chase but calm for all that. 'Tell him I want to talk to him.'

Colley gestured to Blizzard who, blowing hard, managed to regain his breath and walked with heavy foot along the harbour to where David Prendergast had now clambered on top of the harbour wall and was balancing precariously.

'The game's up,' said Blizzard, still wheezing. 'There's nowhere to go, David.'

He noticed that Prendergast still held the hat. The coat had been dropped as he fled across the wasteland and one of the uniformed officers had stayed behind to ensure it remained undisturbed for the forensics team.

'Perhaps there is somewhere to go,' said Prendergast, glancing down into the dark waters on the far side of the harbour wall.

'Don't do anything stupid,' said Blizzard, taking a step forward.

'Stay there,' said Prendergast, holding up a hand.

'We can't stand here all night,' said Blizzard. 'Come down. Daniel needs you.'

'The last thing he needs is a father in prison,' said Prendergast with a bitter laugh. 'My sister in Leeds will look after him and my father will help her.'

'What kind of a life would that be for him?' protested Blizzard.

'At least it'll be a life. Olly did not even get that.'

'Come on,' said Blizzard, holding out a hand. 'Your father has told us what happened – we know Eddie Barton was killed in the heat of the moment and that Stoddart killed Colclough. Which just leaves Moody and a jury might even go for manslaughter with diminished responsibility on him....'

'Diminished responsibility,' said Prendergast drily, 'that's a laugh. Whose diminished responsibility, Chief Inspector? The teachers who failed to stop the drug dealing, the police officers who did not arrest the boys who took my Olly's life? They certainly did not show much responsibility.'

'We can work this out,' said Blizzard, his hand still extended.

'I don't think so.'

'Please,' said Blizzard urgently, 'think of Daniel. He still needs you, David. What would jumping achieve for him?

You're still his father, prison or not. And he will still love you. Olly is dead, his mother is dead, what good are you if you are dead?'

'What good am I alive?' said Prendergast bitterly. 'I couldn't protect his brother, could I?'

'But Daniel is alive – that has got to count for something, surely?'

The comment seemed to hit Prendergast hard and he was silent for a moment or two. Then he nodded and took a step forward along the harbour wall. But he stopped short of jumping down on to the path, preferring instead to glance backwards and take a lingering look across the river at the lights of the chemical works, a view that Blizzard knew so well. Prendergast seemed to realize it was the last time he would see it for a long time.

'Maybe you're right,' he said at length.

'And we've got Ransome anyway,' said Blizzard. 'You can't get him anyway.'

'He's a lucky boy,' said Prendergast looking over the river again. 'He gets to live.'

'And so can you.'

'Maybe.'

'Ransome will be charged with Derek Stoddart's murder,' said Blizzard, desperate to keep him talking and acutely conscious of Colley and a small knot of officers some metres further back down the path, eyeing the conversation intently. 'We are pretty sure we can prove that. He'll go to prison for life.'

'He deserves it.'

'How did they find out Derek was the Vengeance Man?' asked Blizzard.

'Billy Thompson must have let it slip,' said Prendergast absent-mindedly, his eyes seemingly drawn to the scene across the river. 'That's when they went after him. After he had been shot, I knew it had gone too far.'

'But you still killed Moody?'

Prendergast shrugged.

'Rules of the game,' he said.

'Well, the game has to end here,' said Blizzard firmly, having kept his hand extended throughout the confrontation. 'We can sort this out, if only for Daniel's sake.'

An image of his young son in his mind and his decision made, Prendergast nodded, gave a crooked smile and put the hat on at a jaunty angle. A last act of defiance from a man breaking up inside. He took a step forward along the wall but as he did so, his foot slipped on a mossy patch and with a horrified cry he lost his balance. Within the blink of an eye, he had gone, plunging into the deep waters. Blizzard and Colley raced to the railings and peered down but there was no sight of him. The sergeant threw off his coat and raced along to the ladder leading down to the boats and they heard him hurl himself into the water. Within seconds, two other officers had stripped off and followed him but within a few minutes, the icy waters forced them to abandon their brave efforts to save him.

It was only as he drove slowly home that night, having spent a painful hour with a heartbroken Albert Prendergast, that John Blizzard realized with a jolt that he had not heard a splash when his son hit the water.

CHAPTER **THIRTY-ONE**

Seven months later John Blizzard stood at his favourite spot on the river one early summer night and stared out over towards the chemical plant. It had been a tiring and stressful day; after a ten-day trial Raymond Ransome had been jailed for life for the murder of Derek Stoddart, the attempted murder of the shop-keeper shot in the leg, who eventually recovered, and his involvement in the other armed robberies. After that initial interview with Blizzard and Colley, Ransome had never said another word to the police but there was enough evidence to convict him anyway. Gradually piecing together the story, the police were able to tell the jury that Ransome was a major part of the gang, heavily involved in the planning and execution of their crimes. His mother Pauline, sitting in the dock, sobbed throughout the foreman's verdict and the judge's comments. Blizzard wondered cynically if it was for a lost son or the loss of face among the other parents. The judge concluded by commending police, including Blizzard, Colley, and Ramsey for their work in painstakingly compiling the case and securing the conviction. When the judge uttered those words, Blizzard had nodded at the DI. Ramsey allowed himself a slight smile.

For Blizzard, what had happened bore a certain irony, a word that kept cropping up, thought the chief inspector. David Prendergast, a decent man driven bad, who ordinarily would have supported the police, had ended up dead while a scumbag like Ransome got to live, thanks to the police he reviled. Blizzard was not quite sure if that was justice or not.

There was another trial connected to the case: Billy Thompson had been convicted of perverting the course of justice and jailed for six months, suspended dependent on him attending a drug rehabilitation clinic. Blizzard had snorted when he heard the judgement but was pleased that he had achieved another conviction; for all the detective had solved the case, the two killers had died before being arrested and it looked better if at least a couple of people ended up standing in a dock.

The only other legal decision made was whether or not to charge Albert Prendergast for covering up his son's activities. In the end, quietly and away from the media glare that had surrounded the case, the old man was cautioned but never taken to court. The CPS had told Blizzard that, given his age and the sharp deterioration in his health since his son's death, it was not really in the public's interest to prosecute. Blizzard had nodded and said nothing but inside he was cheering.

He knew that Daniel and his grandfather had been broken by the incident and they went to live with the teenager's aunt in Leeds – as the boy's father had planned. By coincidence, on the afternoon following the end of the Ransome trial, the inquest into David Prendergast was held, delayed because the body had still not turned up, the marine unit telling the coroner that the thick reeds along the river sometimes kept corpses concealed for many months, sometimes for ever. Deciding that further delay was pointless, the coroner held the inquest and cleared police of any blame.

Daniel's aunt had attended the hearing and told reporters after the death by misadventure verdict that, although she acknowledged that what her brother had done was wrong, he had acted for the noblest of reasons. She felt, she said with passion as she gave an interview outside the courthouse, that many other people could be held responsible for her brother's death and that of his son Olly. Standing nearby, John Blizzard could do nothing but silently agree although he had vanished by the time the reporters turned to elicit a comment from him and it was left to Arthur Ronald to say the right things.

As Blizzard drove home from the court, he turned on the radio and gave a dry laugh when he heard that Hafton City Council had announced the closure of Heston Comprehensive School, citing falling rolls, the need to make financial cutbacks and concerns over pupil discipline. Mervyn Howatch's greatest fear – apart from the cancer that turned out not to exist – that they would take away his school, had been realized. Not that he was there to see it; he had taken early retirement and had not set foot in a school since. There was even a rumour that he and his wife had left the city. As for John Pendrie, Blizzard insisted that CID investigate him and although he was never charged for his cannabis use – it was never proved he smoked it in school hours – he was cautioned about his future conduct and the education authority sacked him a few weeks before the closure announcement.

As for Heston, things returned to normal, the drug dealers had all but gone and the residents returned to their quiet and trim everyday lives. Marty Cundall turned up eventually and was now on bail while Ramsey's team questioned him about matters that emerged in interviews conducted during the Vengeance Man inquiry. Chris Ramsey was, as Blizzard had predicted, attracting plenty of attention as he rigorously led the investigation and there were even some who talked of him as a future Regional Crime Squad officer. Some even whispered that he might become a detective chief inspector – but not within Blizzard's hearing. Even the chief constable had taken a keen interest in the inquiry and had invited Ramsey to his office to give him a personal briefing. Blizzard allowed himself a gentle smile at this. As he told Ronald, he loved it when a plan came together.

As for Robert Stanshall, the Vengeance Man brought his world crashing around his ears. Embittered about the whole affair, Bob Chatterton went to the media and leaked the story about the plans for the Vengeance Man theme park ride. Although Stanshall had long since abandoned the plan, the publicity was highly damaging to his reputation, the families of the dead teenagers protesting and the council announcing that it was reviewing the planning permission for the theme park. Stanshall, shocked by the vigour of the criticism and the dramatic drop in visitor numbers that followed, closed the park, which now stood silent and lifeless, its rides eerily quiet and deserted. He retreated behind his wrought iron gates then one day was gone, putting the house on the market and heading for his villa in Spain. Few expected to see him back. And his son never gave that statement to the police.

Now, beside the river, Blizzard reflected on the events of the past seven months as he stared out across the dark waters.

'So many lives,' he said softly, 'no winners.'

A crunching sound behind him made him turn round and he smiled as Colley walked across the shingle.

'Thought I'd find you here,' said the sergeant.

'I like it here. Peaceful….'

'Yes, but there's one thing missing.'

'Which is?' asked Blizzard bleakly.

'A pub.'

Blizzard chuckled and clapped his sergeant on the shoulder.

'I seem to recall that there's a nice little boozer on Heston Market Place,' said the chief inspector. 'Come on, I'll buy you a pint….'

'You know, guv,' grinned Colley as they walked up the foreshore towards the car park, 'you do say the nicest things.'

EPILOGUE

Later that night, a fisherman returning late from a trip with a group of sea anglers, ploughing through the choppy waters of the Haft and guided by the beam of the full moon, noticed a dark shape floating past.

Suspecting it to be a body, he tried to grab it but it twisted in the current and slipped from his grasp to head silently, noiselessly, past the disused docks with their skeletal cranes, past the trendy riverside apartments, past the gleaming glass-fronted business parks, and out towards the open sea.